PRAISE FOR TRACE

"Letitia Moffitt has a winner with Trace! She blends police procedural, supernatural thriller, and romance with a skill which as a writer I admired and as a reader I enjoyed enormously. An engaging protagonist, a deepening mystery, and great pacing add up to a terrifically entertaining read."

— Frank Chadwick, author of *How Dark the World Becomes*

"In Letitia Moffitt's gripping new mystery, Nola is a female detective with a unique gift who finds herself dropped into her first case—a case that seems to have a lot of questions, even more suspects, and zero answers. Moffitt's writing is utterly engaging right from the first page. I couldn't put it down. If you like Megan Abbott's style of new noir, then you will absolutely love *Trace*."

— Tommy Zurhellen, author of *Armageddon, Texas*

"Trace is funny and engaging, and best of all, a page-turner. Mystery meets paranormal in Moffitt's big-hearted heroine, Nola. Wholly believable—when you're done, you'll wonder where the tracists have been hiding all this time."
— Lania Knight, author of *Three Cubic Feet*

"Moffitt draws a compelling accidental heroine in Nola Lantri, a no-nonsense, crime-solving 'tracist' who struggles to be normal despite her paranormal abilities."
— Jeff Kohmstedt, author of *The Fifth Kraut*

"*Trace* is a wonderful novel—entertaining and suspenseful with a fascinating premise and pitch-perfect writing. What I love most is Nola Lantri, the smart, steely, and often sarcastic heroine who holds her own in a masculine world. More Nola Lantri books, please!"
— Daiva Markelis, author of *White Field, Black Sheep: A Lithuanian-American Life*

PRAISE FOR VIBE/SYNC

"I loved *Vibe/Sync*! Nola Lantri is back along with a slew of fascinating characters, some merely odd, some deliciously creepy, and a few downright evil. As in *Trace*, the writing is razor sharp and the plot highly suspenseful. I started reading this wonderful novel and couldn't put it down."
— Daiva Markelis, author of *White Field, Black Sheep: A Lithuanian-American Life*

"Letitia Moffitt returns to her TraceWorld series, giving us two new stories under one cover, two dramatically different new characters with two new paranormal talents, and so expands the scope of her world enormously. But Moffitt's original engaging heroine, Nola Lantri, remains the glue which holds the stories together with wit and courage."
— Frank Chadwick, author of *How Dark the World Becomes*

"Fellow Trace fans, we can now rejoice: Nola Lantri is back in *Vibe/Sync*, the second novel in Letitia Moffitt's ground-breaking para-thriller series . . . *Vibe/Sync* surprises with multiple points-of-view and plot twists that make this second book even better than the first. From the first page to the very last, I couldn't put this one down."

    — Tommy Zurhellen, author of *Armageddon, Texas*

"Moffitt does it again with *Vibe/Sync*, and Emjay is a perfect character to pull you back into the Trace world. Emjay is sharp, she's conflicted, and she has a killer to catch."

    — Jeff Kohmstedt, author of *The Fifth Kraut*

Moffitt's writing, with its controlled energy, reads much like the supernatural abilities of her characters. *Vibe/Sync* gets under the skin, under the surface of the human performance. Like the newly-detected chirp of gravitational waves, this novel will surprise readers with its echoes, questions, and wildly suspenseful ending.

    — Catherine Zobal Dent, author of *Unfinished Stories of Girls*

"Returning to the TraceWorld series, Letitia Moffitt expands Nola Lantri's investigations with new characters, new abilities, and new adventures. Clever, inventive, and engaging, *Vibe/Sync* is a book that delights."

    — Tawnysha Greene, author of *A House Made of Stars*

Vibe/Sync

Cantraip Press, Ltd.
2317 Saratoga Pl.
Charleston, Illinois 61920

www.cantraip.com

Publisher's Note: This is a work of fiction. Names, characters, places, and incidents are a product of the author's imagination. Locales and public names are sometimes used for atmospheric purposes. Any resemblance to actual people, living or dead, or to businesses, companies, events, institutions, or locales is completely coincidental.

Cover Design by damonza.com
Vibe/Sync / Letitia L. Moffitt -- 1st ed.
Paperback ISBN 978-1-942737-06-3
Electronic ISBN 978-1-942737-07-0
LCCN 2016935352

Vibe/Sync

TraceWorld Book 2

Letitia L. Moffit

Cantraip Press

Vibe

1

THE SHIVERING CHIHUAHUA STARED mournfully at Eric Lafferty from a woman's shoulder bag in front of him on the subway platform. Dogs were to blame for the sad state of his life. They weren't directly the cause of his unhappiness, of course, but if he hadn't read that damned article when he was sixteen, things would have been different. He would have . . . he wouldn't have . . . and here he had to stop and be honest with himself. Would have what? Stayed in the miserable little town of his childhood bullied by his father? Instead he'd gotten away, taken a chance. The chance hadn't paid off, and now he was going back. The trembling critter sneezed, or seemed to, and resumed fixing its oversized eyes on Eric's. At least he wasn't going back to be bullied again, merely to pay pretend respects to the dearly departed former bully James Lafferty, dead two weeks. Rest in peace, asshole. He nodded grimly at the dog.

The article had been about some scientist's hypothesis that dogs, with their acute hearing, were able to sense the brainwaves of human beings, which accounted in part for why they often seemed so in tune with their owners' emotional states. The part about brainwaves was valid; brains actually gave off waves, and in theory, as with any wave, they could be "heard." Eric didn't care about the dog part, since he'd never had one—his father had said, to his face, that Eric was "too much of a retard" to take care of a pet. It was the part about hearing brain waves that made him pay attention. He experienced one of those "click" moments. Suddenly everything made sense.

Down at the far end of the crowded platform, a man and a woman, dressed punkishly, conversed in ASL. Eric let his attention wander from the sickly looking dog to their conversation, following bits and pieces of it. They were animated in their signs even though they weren't saying much that was terribly dramatic, at least what fragments he could catch. *Last night . . . at the party . . . fuck him . . . fuck her . . . fuck . . .* something else that made them laugh hysterically. He was getting rusty. He'd studied ASL years ago in college just for the hell of it. Why not? For a long time his childhood doctors had thought he might be deaf. He looked at people so oddly when they spoke to him, like he wasn't really looking at them but off to the side. "The side" wasn't a place but an idea in his head. He wasn't deaf; he was just listening to something else. Voices, speech, these didn't interest him nearly as much as the other sounds he heard. Another language came from the people who tried to get him to communicate, but he was the only one who heard it. The language was their thoughts. He was reading their minds.

In the movies mind-readers heard people's thoughts in perfect English, in their speaking voices. Eric heard just sound, vibrations. It was brain waves he was hearing, after all. And just because he heard them didn't mean, at least at first, that he understood them at all. His initial lack of comprehension was compounded by the fact that the people speaking this "language" didn't understand it either—couldn't even hear themselves speaking it. That only made it more compelling to him. After reading that ridiculous little article, he'd found his purpose in life. He felt like an archaeologist discovering an ancient language. No one else on earth understood that language, no one communicated in it anymore, and the people who had communicated in it were long dead and could not speak back to him—or to each other. Despite all this, he had been determined to master it.

As he listened to the hum of vibrations from the platform, he felt a small, quick shift. People turned their heads to the right. The train was coming. At that moment Eric wanted to laugh as hysterically as the ASL couple, only without any trace of pleasure. Everyone else was listening for the train. He was listening to them listen for the train. As a result, everyone else knew it was coming before he did, and he'd gained nothing, not one damn thing, from doing what he did.

The train pulled in, the doors opened, and the crowd shuffled and shoved, bumped and nudged. As he stood surrounded by the nearly tangible wall of their vibes, Eric glanced around discreetly once again, as he often did in crowds, looking for something recognizable even if he'd never seen it before. He'd always supposed there had to be other people able to read vibes, as he termed it. But supposing he somehow met one and knew he was meeting one, what did it matter? Vibes weren't really a language, so it wasn't like he could talk to other vibe readers any better than anyone else. They might understand him better, but that was all. They would know he wasn't deaf (how many times did the doctors have to clap their hands behind him to see if he turned around?) or autistic or "retarded." His father's word.

Funny, he reflected, glancing at the disheveled wino on a seat near to him. The man didn't stink or act drunk, but everyone knew, and no one else wanted to sit next to him. Eric often wondered if his own father heard vibes, which might have been a reason for the alcoholism that killed the old man. Drown out the noise so no one will think you're a retard. It's OK to turn your liver into a toxic waste dump and verbally abuse your wife and child at every opportunity—that's socially acceptable for a man—but not to sit quietly and listen. Whether this had been true about James Lafferty, Eric would never know, and even if his father were still alive, he would never ask. He knew his mother was torn up about the fact that father and son had never reconciled. Eric wished he could assuage this particular grief, but the only comfort he could offer was to tell her it was better that her husband was dead. Somehow he didn't think that would help.

It was better that his father was dead because otherwise Eric would have to admit to the old man that he was wasting his own young life, no better than an aimless drifter for the past decade. He had wanted to make something of himself, something great, with his odd ability. He had failed spectacularly.

Despite the crush of bodies, the car was surprisingly quiet, in vibes and in voices. It was early. Eric hated wasting a whole day flying, so he'd taken a night flight from SFO to LaGuardia and gotten in at ridiculous o'clock. Now he had a couple of hours to kill before the Amtrak to Albany left Penn Station. It would only take him half of that to get into Manhattan, and he'd brought nothing to read and there was nothing interesting to hear. Early morning crowds were always so steady and dull, their vibes still half asleep. No, that wasn't true. Dreamers' vibes, the few times Eric had gotten close enough to someone sleeping to hear them, were often crazed and vivid. He smiled remembering the last time he'd heard someone's dreams. He didn't know her name, wasn't even sure of the color of her eyes, but he knew exactly the moment she'd turned her full attention to him in that noisy bar, and even though he hadn't heard the flirty line she gave him, he knew what she wanted.

His smile hardened into wryness. Ten years of studying a language and the only useful thing he learned was how to get lucky once in a while. He supposed that would be enough for most people. It might have to be enough for him. He glanced down at the two pretty women seated nearby, one of whom held a folded-up newspaper and was gesturing toward it. Despite the circumstances of his return, he liked being back in New York. Broadway shows, world-class museums, Michelin-starred restaurants, and yet people still got newsprint on their fingers every morning like the residents of this metropolis had for over a century.

Their vibes weren't telling him anything useful (like whether they'd noticed him), so he reluctantly eavesdropped on their conversation. Apparently some girl from a rich Manhattan family was in the news. The news wasn't good. *Found the body . . . upstate, not here . . . at first they thought . . . not suicide, though . . . murder . . . so tragic . . . so young . . . ran away from home . . . part of some cult, they say . . . think the cult members killed her . . . someone named Anna.*

At that moment, the vibes directly behind him changed. A hard pulsing beat. Loud. Fast. A reaction to what one of the women had just said. Before he could stop himself, Eric turned sharply around.

A tall man in an expensive suit stood there. He was not staring at the women but he didn't have to be. After a lifetime of listening to vibes, Eric still understood very little, but there was one thing he never got wrong: no matter how poker-faced people might appear, he always knew when something got their attention. The murder had caught this man's attention.

And now Eric had caught it as well.

The man turned his head sharply to meet Eric's eyes.

Shock, confusion—and guilt. Vibes usually felt as benign as a tuning fork, but this man's vibes pounded at Eric like a battering ram to his solar plexus. He'd been caught in something, Eric had no idea what, and the man had no idea how he could have been caught. Whatever reason he had for suddenly paying attention to the women's conversation, Eric's attention had thrown him off balance. They locked eyes; neither moved. Eric seldom listened to his own vibes—it was like hearing your own heartbeat; you could tune it out easily—but all he could hear was the sound of his own absolute terror. Then the man stepped toward him.

The train shuddered to a stop and the doors slid open. Eric bolted from the train.

Halfway up the platform stairs, he knew without turning around that the man was following him.

He burst through the turnstile, took the exit stairs by twos, and leapt out onto the sidewalk without a clue where he was or where he was going. For a few seconds he stood immobile. Then he heard it: those hard, determined vibes behind him. Eric ran.

Shit. What was happening? What was this? And what was he supposed to do? Call the cops? He couldn't, even if he wanted to. He'd never owned a cellphone, hated phones in general, hated listening to disembodied voices. He couldn't understand people properly unless he heard their vibes along with their voices, and that didn't happen on the phone. He didn't even have anything on him that he could pretend was a phone so that the man would think he was calling the cops. And there were no pay phones. Of course not. They'd just get vandalized, and anyway, *normal* people had their own phones.

He had to find a cop. If the man saw him talking to a cop, there was no way he'd come near. Eric wouldn't even have to say anything of substance to the cop—and what could he say anyway? *Officer, this man following me may be a murderer, and how I know it, see, is that I... I can... I'm...*

A retard. That's what my father thought. He's dead now, but I don't intend to follow in his footsteps any time soon.

Newsstands, bus stops, clumps of tourists, suited office workers. Eric dodged and dashed, his eyes looking for one thing only, that one particular shade of blue. He'd never held the police in high esteem before this—like most young white men, he reckoned, he had the privilege of being able to regard them as little more than a minor nuisance. When he turned a corner—the corner of some avenue and street, he didn't know which or what—and saw a female officer just ahead pitching a coffee cup into the trash, he nearly wept with joy. He tried to compose himself so that he didn't look like a madman, but as soon as he approached he could hear her vibes become alert.

"Sir?"

He panted, more from his emotional state than the exertion of the run, and tried to speak. Conversation had always been difficult for him; he was so used to listening to other people that he sometimes failed to realize he was expected to respond. "Ah . . . Penn Station? I'm, er, lost. Got off at the wrong stop. I, uh, don't want to miss my train."

The cop stared silently at him for a moment, the way cops did, before he sensed her on-guard sensibilities ease. A faint smile played on her lips. "You sure did get off at the wrong stop. You're about twelve blocks off. That way." She gestured with her chin down the street the way Eric had come.

He looked. The man was at the end of the block, watching them. He looked, of all things, puzzled. Not wary, not scared of being caught, just confused, as though he himself suddenly realized he was lost in the city. Then he turned and walked away.

The cop was still staring fixedly at Eric, so before she could question him he babbled thanks, trying to speak and smile and act like a normal person, and headed in the direction she'd indicated—slowly. He knew his retreat from her must have looked even crazier than his approach—if he was so worried about missing his train, why had his pace slowed to a crawl?—but he needed to make sure all was clear. When he got to the corner, he peered up the avenue. The man was gone.

The vibes of eight million people hummed around him. He ignored them. He just wanted out of the city. For the first time ever, Eric relished the thought of going home.

2

W HEN ERIC TOLD PEOPLE he'd left home at seventeen and hadn't been back since, it always sounded more dramatic than it needed to be. After all, he'd left to go to college, and because college was on the west coast and his folks lived in upstate New York, he couldn't afford to return. Of course this was in part because his father refused to give Eric any money, not even to come back for the holidays, even though his mother longed for a reunion. No, thought Eric, far better to spend that money rotting his liver than coddling his son. That was James Lafferty reasoning for you.

Most of Eric's college classmates had far more money than he did, and he felt it, but he certainly couldn't claim to be the only hard-luck story around. There were plenty of students on full scholarship and still having to work to get by. None of them, at least as far as he knew, had chosen Eric's particular method of getting by.

Vibe reading was most useful when people's exterior demeanor—how they behaved—was at odds with their interior state—their vibes. After doing some digging, Eric finally got himself into the high-stakes poker circuit (high stakes for college students in the Bay Area, anyway). He figured he had an advantage no one else did and no one else could ever discover: he would know when the other players were bluffing. But picking up vibes didn't give him quite the advantage he initially expected. He soon learned that most hard-core poker players were always bluffing in one way or another. He had to change his strategy, and as it turned out, this ended up giving him a bigger advantage than he'd originally thought.

Poker required two things: the ability to quickly calculate the odds of success for a given hand, and the ability to read other players. The first part could easily be learned. The second part was the key—or at least what most players saw as the key. At first he could only tell if someone drew an exceptionally strong hand. Because it happened so rarely and it meant not bluffing in quite the same way, players couldn't easily control their brief blip of surprise. Even if their face didn't show it, their vibes gave it away. This didn't help Eric actually win more, but it was enough of an advantage to help him stay in the game.

Eric's other advantage was not caring much what he had in his own hand. The truly exceptional players realized there was a third component: keeping everyone else from reading you yourself. If you're busy concentrating on discovering another player's tells, you might not realize you're revealing your own. Eric didn't have to bother with any of that. By barely glancing at his cards, this risk was lessened considerably. It didn't much matter how good or bad his hand was; what mattered was whether someone at the table had an exceptionally good hand. Eric was tempted to play a game without ever looking at his cards, but that might give too much away—or, rather, might lead the other players to suspect he was cheating.

From there on, the longer he played with a group of people, the more familiar he became with their vibe patterns. It was a little like each player had his own musical scale. *The man in the Oakland Raiders baseball cap is C minor; when he has a bad hand, it registers as C or D, but when it's better, it goes to G or A flat.* Of course there weren't really sounds accompanying the vibes, but the analogy kept Eric's conscious mind in sync with the vibe-reading part of his brain. He only had to pay attention to the moments after a deal, their initial reaction to the cards, not what followed. In the split second it took good players to comprehend how good their hand was, Eric also comprehended it. They might as well have laid their cards face up on the table.

His "system" wasn't perfect—he often lost a lot of early hands deliberately in order to read the others—but he won considerably more often than he lost. He developed a bit of a reputation. Some other players won just as often, but Eric's demeanor at the table was so odd that no one could figure out what he was doing. He barely glanced at his cards and, more perplexing, never seemed to look up at other players. How in the world was he doing it? How could he know to push a bluffing player to the limit if he wasn't trying to read the bluff? This reputation only helped; he was invited to a lot of games by ever-better players, all seeking to best him.

Poker also taught him something he hadn't been able to learn in any other way: how to interact. Sometimes he experimented in the early rounds to test the reactions. What would happen if he suddenly aggressively began to bet his head off, as though he either had phenomenal cards or had nothing but phenomenal bluffing chutzpah? What would happen if he acted nervous and hesitant? He began to transfer these experiments to his non-poker life, with mostly positive results. People were uncomfortable with his inert silence as he tried to get their vibes. When he put on some kind of act, they felt more secure, more sure of the situation. They thought they understood him.

He let them think that. It made life so much easier.

THE YOUNG WOMAN WHO picked him up at the train station didn't seem terribly happy to see him, though given that she'd never seen him before, he figured she must be having a bad day. His mother disliked driving on the interstate, and while one could get to Albany from Redfort using back-roads, it took forever. Fortunately, his mother had informed him, her neighbor was going to Albany that very day—"a lovely girl, Nola, about your age," which was his mother's non-subtle way of suggesting he should date this lovely girl, propose to her, marry her, and settle down in Redfort for-ever, as if that wasn't the stuff of his worst nightmares.

Lovely Nola wore a frown and her vibes were jangling. She did, however, match his mother's description of her, so he approached, trying not to stare too hard—not be-cause she was attractive (she was, in fact, with a trim figure and hair he wanted to smell, if that weren't such a creepy thought), but because he always stared at people when he met them, always tried to get a fix on their mental states. Inevitably their mental states changed before he could get that fix, and all he'd learned over the years was that most people hated being stared at.

Nola was no exception. "Um, hello?" she said, her voice sharp. "Eric Lafferty?" He merely nodded, and her vibes, voice, and face softened. "Sorry. I'm not having a good day. C'mon, the car's out front. Hope the train ride was OK. Your mother is …"

She stopped walking. Eric stopped too. Their faces might have been mirrors of astonishment. What prompted Nola's astonishment Eric didn't know, but his own was from her vibes. They were disappearing. They were going silent as if she were dying before his eyes—but she clearly wasn't dying.

She was breathing hard, her fist clenched around her car keys so hard he thought she might crush them.

"Oh shit. The jumper." She glanced over at him at last. "I forgot about that. I guess you wouldn't have heard. There was a jumper on this platform a few months back. A teenage boy. Jumped in front of the train." Now she studied his face closely. "You don't know, do you? Guess your mother didn't tell you much about me."

Eric was pretty sure his mother hadn't told Nola anything about him either. What was *her* "not told" thing?

Nola inhaled, exhaled, then resumed walking toward the platform exit. It was more like marching than walking, actually, and Eric scrambled to keep up. "I'm what's called a tracist. When the human body expires, it leaves an energy trace behind. Some people are able to sense this trace, just like how some people are able to hear at very high or low ranges, or have extremely sensitive taste buds." She spoke in a practiced manner and kept her tone neutral and steady, like the narrator of some educational film. Eric marveled at that; he'd never been able to explain so clearly and authoritatively what it was like for him with vibes. Of course, he seldom ever tried explaining it. Clearly tracism was a known thing, and Nola was "out" about it. He wanted to laugh at that. He used to admire and even envy the people he knew back in California who were gay and out; they would probably be harassed all their lives for it, maybe even worse, but at least they didn't have to pretend any more. Their interactions with the world didn't have to be experiments. They could say *This is who I am* and be proud of it. Despite the weirdness of her moment on the platform, Nola seemed able to do that.

None of this explained what had happened to her vibes. Perhaps, Eric thoughts churned in the silence of the car, perhaps when she sensed this trace, it blocked out her other vibes? Trace was death energy, after all, or so he assumed based on her brief explanation. He wanted to know more. He wanted to ask her about it. He couldn't, though. It felt too much like an invasion of privacy—not hers, but his own. She would probably answer anything he asked, but he was afraid to betray his curiosity, afraid to show interest, lest that interest be turned back on him. After a lifetime of tuning in on people's thoughts, he had no idea how to share them openly.

Nola did not appear to have that problem. After some time had passed (how much, he had no idea) with not a word exchanged, she glanced at him, hesitated, then spoke. "I'm sorry about your father."

The words were soft, gentle, kind—even he could perceive that—but they still fell like a bomb. "I'm not," he blurted so violently that she physically and mentally recoiled from him. Well, he wasn't sorry, and he didn't care who knew it, though as his rage waned— the rage he felt whenever his father was mentioned—it occurred to him that she might have been embarrassed for herself, at having referred to something personal to a near-stranger. He want-ed to assure her it wasn't her fault; she'd merely said what people said in these situations. She couldn't know—well, anything at all, really, about his past.

When she spoke next, her tone was chatty. "So. Wanna hear about my bad day?" Without waiting for an answer, she continued. "So I was in Albany today to help out a friend—er, more like an acquaintance. Actually I barely know her, and it seemed very weird that she asked me to help her out. Anyway, she has this new-agey sort of store out near the uni-versity. Crystals and candles and stuff that might be edible or might not, I was never sure. I do the organic local thing and I recycle and all that, but there are things in that store that look like they come from another planet. And she wanted me to run the place for a couple of days. I have the time—I'm on paid leave from my job—so I figured why not."

She paused for a moment, and Eric found himself nod-ding at her to continue. She had an engaging storyteller's voice that made him cease staring moodily out the window at the bleak November landscape and wait to hear more. "She had to go out of town, she said—something had sud-denly come up. She needed me to run the store and do a few other, uh, errands for her."

The way she said "errands" piqued his curiosity. Had the friend turned out to be a drug dealer? A call girl? A hit woman? As though reading his mind (ha-ha, he thought with a smirk), she said, "What errands, right? And why me?

Well, this woman is also a tracist. That's how we met. Well, sort of. Anyway, she has these . . . I don't know what you'd call them, gigs, I guess, where she uses her tracism to make money." Nola chuckled. "Boy, does that sound cynical. I don't mean that she's some shyster. I mean—well, for example, at lunchtime I had to go with this realtor who represents these very wealthy, very superstitious people who want to buy an old mansion in the historic district and refurbish it. Anna works as a consultant with people like this the way feng shui experts do: goes in and makes sure there's no 'bad trace' lingering around the house."

"Was there? In the mansion, I mean."

"Oh, hell yeah, there was. Plenty of it. Stale, some of it, but there. Seemed like whole generations of rich folks must've died there." She grinned and then laughed outright. "At least that's the story I told the realtor. I may have been exaggerating slightly. There was trace, but just a little. But I'd had a tough morning selling seaweed tea and vegan Jell-o, and I felt like messing with the guy's head. You should have seen the expression on his face. Mortification can't even begin to describe it. He'd probably already been planning how he was going to spend the big fat check his clients were going to present him at the end of the sale, and now he had to tell them their little refurbishing project was haunted."

She laughed again. So did Eric. At that moment, he realized they'd entered Redfort—a moment when the last thing he'd expected to be doing was laughing.

"So after that I went back to the granola stand and ran the place until closing, and just when I was about to turn the sign around from open to close, this group of people came in all at once looking for Anna. They wouldn't leave, even when I told them she wasn't there and I didn't know where she was. Four of 'em, just standing there, all pale-faced and serious as heart attacks. Finally I had to go to pick you up, so I said," and here she paused for effect, "'Folks, I'd love to stick around but I'm late for a funeral.'" Nola shrugged. "It was sort of true, right?"

In truth the funeral had been last week—he'd given his mother a fairly half-assed excuse for missing it—but that wasn't what was he was thinking about. In his periphery he saw Nola glance anxiously at him, perhaps afraid she'd offended him again, but it wasn't that either. He was looking up the street—they were coming close to where his mother lived—at a man waiting outside his mother's apartment.

It was the man from the train, leaning against a car while typing into his phone. How could he be here?

"Turn the car around," he whispered—as though the man could hear him.

Nola looked sharply at him. "What?"

"Turn the car around. Keep driving. Do not stop. Go!"

She did as he said.

3

"**P**ULL OVER HERE."

Nola pulled into a side street and stopped. Eric waited, eyes fixed on the side-view mirror. When several minutes had passed and the car he'd seen did not appear, he exhaled and sat up, barely aware he'd hunched down low in his seat. He stared at the dashboard, not sure what to say next.

"You OK?" Nola said gently. He looked unwillingly at her and was surprised to see only concern, not creeped-out wariness. "I know this has got to be tough for you, your dad and all. Not to get too personal or anything but, well, I know what he was like."

It took Eric a confused moment to realize she must have thought he'd freaked out when he saw the apartment because he didn't want to face the past. Being his parents' neighbor, this woman must have known what his father was

like, must have seen his mother shamefully taking the emp-
ties to the recycling bin, heard the curses, and witnessed the
ugliness of the last days of James Lafferty's life. Of course
she had no idea what had happened in New York that morning. How had the man found out where Eric was going?
How had he beat them? It was technically possible for the
guy to drive straight from Manhattan to Redfort far faster
than it took Eric to get to Albany by train and Nola to drive
them to Redfort, but it still meant that the man knew where
they were going. How was that possible? More important,
why was he here?

Of more immediate concern, how on earth could he explain all of this to Nola?

"No, it isn't that. There was a man outside your building.
Did you see him?"

Now Nola looked confused. "I didn't notice. I was waiting for that stupid Cadillac to clear the intersection so I
could make the left turn. Who was this guy? You know him?"

"Sort of." He sighed, glancing once more in the side-
view mirror. Despite the urgency, he did not want to do
this, but he couldn't see a way out of it. He inhaled deeply
again and then spoke in a blurted rush. "OK. You know the
thing you told me about being a tracist? I've got something
like that, only what I have doesn't have a name. I can hear
brain waves. I don't always know what they mean, but I
can hear them as clearly as speech. This morning in Manhattan, something happened. These women on the subway

were talking about the murder of a teenage girl that had just happened—I don't know if you heard about it." In his periphery he saw Nola nod. He couldn't face her directly. He hated talking about vibes and dreaded her reaction. And yet he wanted to look at her again. "This man was on the train—the man outside your apartment—and as soon as he heard them talking about the murder, I heard him—his vibes, his brainwaves—reacting. Strongly, especially when the girl's name was mentioned. And when I turned to look at him, he saw me looking. I guess, I don't know, maybe I sort of freaked him out. When I got off the train, he followed me. And now he's here."

"So, are you thinking he might be involved in the murder somehow? Did you get a good look at his car? Could you identify him again?"

Eric now stared right at her, trying to keep his jaw from dropping open. Her large dark eyes focused on his as she waited for him to answer. She hadn't missed a beat, hadn't edged away from him, had listened to everything he said and taken it seriously. Who was this person? "I, uh, didn't get a good look at the car. I've never been good at cars. Him, I can identify. Definitely."

"Good. I think you need to talk to someone I know. I have to meet with him today anyway. I work with the police—well, used to work with them, sometimes, on cases. Anyway, Jack Dalton—he's the Detective Commander—he asked if I could stop by, and—"

"The police?" Eric blurted, annoyed at how his voice cracked. "What the hell am I supposed to say to the police? You really think they're going to buy all this?"

"Well, I did."

You're different, Eric thought. He barely knew this woman, but he knew it was true: Nola was different. Nola understood, somehow. He doubted some spit-and-polish detective would.

"Look, Jack Dalton will listen. He trusted me as a tracist for years when everyone else thought the whole trace business was a joke. If you know something that might help solve a murder, it's worth reporting. Eric, the guy is *here*, in Redfort, looking for you. He's outside your apartment—where your mother lives."

That got his attention. He'd forgotten about his mother. Shame flooded him, and he looked away from her back at the dashboard.

Nola started up the car. "Call your mother," she said quietly. "Tell her you've been delayed a bit but you'll be there soon, so she shouldn't leave the apartment. I'll drive us to the police station."

"I don't have a phone," Eric mumbled, his shame rising.

Nola handed him hers, then pulled the car out onto the main road and headed downtown.

❖

RUGGEDLY HANDSOME—WASN'T THAT HOW people like Jack Dalton were always described? Eric knew he himself would never be described that way. Scruffily moody, one girl in college had called him, or maybe it was moodily scruffy, and that was only because she wanted to sleep with him. Afterward she called him a cold-hearted asshole, which seemed something close to a mixed metaphor, though he'd wisely decided not to point this out to her. In any case, ruggedly handsome Jack Dalton stood before them, smiling warmly at Nola without acknowledging Eric. He might have been her handbag for all the tall commander noticed him.

"Thanks for coming down here on such short notice, Nola." Finally he glanced at Eric, his smile disappearing in an instant, his vibes changing slightly as well. "I'm afraid this is official business."

The implication was clear: get the hell out. Nola spoke quickly. "Jack, this is Eric Lafferty. He's the son of my neighbors. I brought him here because I think he has something important to report about that murdered teen girl."

Jack's vibes shifted again; he looked at Nola with unmistakable admiration. "Now just how did you know I was calling you in about that?" He shook his head. "You are amazing."

"Wait. I didn't know that, Jack. What do you mean? How in the world could I possibly help that case? They already know where she died."

Jack Dalton hesitated, then gestured for both Nola and Eric to follow him to his office. Eric couldn't help feeling foolish and uncomfortable. He had no idea how to explain why he was there. With Nola it had been different—different from how it had been with pretty much everyone else he'd ever spoken to in his life.

"Have you been in contact with Anna Villagomez lately?" the commander asked Nola once they were seated.

The women on the train had said the name "Anna." He'd assumed it was the murdered girl's name. Was there some other Anna involved?

Nola's vibes were surprised as well. "Yes. She called me on Monday and asked if I'd do her a favor and take care of her store as well as a few other, er, jobs she has. I did that today."

"Did she say where she was going?"

"No. Not so much as a hint, and she got a little pissy about it when I asked."

"Did you have any further contact with her?"

"No," Nola said, and Eric felt her grow increasingly agitated. "I thought she was supposed to, but she didn't. Is she connected to the dead girl?"

Jack leaned back in his chair. "There is reason to believe a connection exists. The dead girl—Sabrina Lasky—was known to associate with a group of young men and women, some of them juveniles but most over eighteen, who are suspected to have participated in 'thrill kills' around the Albany area. Two homeless men were strangled and a third asphyxiated in the last three months, all in remote areas. One of the victims and at least two of the suspected gang members are from Redfort, which is why we've been included in the investigation."

Eric was becoming agitated. So the murdered girl was Sabrina, not Anna. What did Anna have to do with any of this?

"Did the gang members kill Sabrina Lasky, too?" Nola asked.

"We don't know. We have reason to believe Lasky wanted to leave the group. The unofficial story is Lasky was a bored little rich girl slumming upstate for fun. She got in with the wrong crowd and got scared."

"So maybe they were afraid she was going to rat them out?"

"That's certainly a possibility."

"What does all this have to do with Anna?"

Eric nodded, seconding Nola's question, though neither Jack nor Nola paid attention to him.

Jack paused, a dramatic effect that irritated Eric. "There is reason to believe Anna has a connection to the group as well."

"What possible connection could ..." Nola stopped, her vibes suddenly jangling. Something, some realization she'd just had, was troubling her deeply. She stared at the commander. "The thrill kill group—were there tracists involved?"

"We have reason to believe that's a possibility."

Eric's head was spinning. He was never much good at following other people's conversations while Nola seemed to have no trouble at all figuring out what was going on, despite her growing agitation. As for Jack Dalton, his repeated use of the royal "we" and his "reasons to believe" grated on Eric so much he could barely focus on the vibes. He realized Nola and Jack were both looking at him. Apparently Nola had tried to bring him into the discussion with a question. She repeated it. "Eric? Could you describe the man you saw outside my building? The one you think has something to do with the murder?" She glanced at Jack Dalton as if to assure him that details would be forthcoming.

Great, thought Eric, *all I have to do is somehow provide the details.* "Um . . . tall. Just about his height." Though it was petty, Eric relished taking Dalton out of the conversation for a change. "Dark brown hair, slightly wavy but short. Blue eyes. Maybe mid-30s, I guess. Expensive suit. Not thin, but not overweight. Athletic-looking, I guess." He paused. What else? Was he carrying anything? Eric couldn't remember. Was there grey in his hair? Scars, moles, anything distinguishing at all? Again, Eric had no idea. The main thing he remembered was the way the man's vibes changed, the way their eyes locked, and the way the man stepped toward him. That was impossible to forget.

Nola and Dalton were silent. For a moment Eric thought they were annoyed he couldn't be more helpful, but then he realized something else was going on. Nola was staring at him and her vibes had changed yet again, this time a hard pulse. She looked at Jack Dalton, who stared back at her, his vibes nearly identical.

Recognition. They knew the man Eric was describing.

Jack Dalton turned to his desktop computer and began typing and clicking. A minute later, he spun the monitor around to Eric. "Is this the man you saw?"

Eric nodded. His gaze dropped to the bottom of the screen, where a name appeared. "Grayson Bryant," he read aloud.

Nola's vibes pounded at him for a few seconds before they calmed. "That explains why he was outside my apartment. He wasn't there for you, Eric. He was there to see me."

"You know him?"

She nodded. "He used to be involved with Anna Villagomez. And—he's a tracist as well."

Now Jack's vibes pulsed surprise. "You never mentioned that. That could be significant."

"How?" Nola challenged him. "You think he and Anna went around killing homeless people to get their trace? You think that's what people like us do in our spare time?"

Jack made a calming gesture with his hands. "I don't think that at all, Nola. At this point we are exploring all possible leads. And thanks to you, we now have a new one." He turned back to Eric. "How did you come to believe Grayson Bryant might be involved with Sabrina Lasky's murder?"

Here it was at last, Eric's moment to be transformed into a freak show. He took a deep breath, found himself holding it, and just when he exhaled and was ready to speak, Nola saved him. "He's sort of a little like a tracist himself. Not exactly the same, but similar. Since you trust me, Jack, you should trust him and not question it."

Her bold tone and confident vibes made Eric almost laugh out loud. Take that, Mr. Ruggedly Handsome. His amusement was short-lived as Jack Dalton turned his attention from Nola to Eric himself. The scrutiny only lasted a few seconds, but they were heavy, hard seconds. Finally Jack turned back to Nola. "That's good enough for me. Thank you, Mr. Lafferty. You've been a huge help."

"Are you going to question Grayson?" Nola said.

"We need to find Anna Villagomez. You don't know where she is; Grayson might."

"If he did, why would he show up at my place? He probably thinks I know."

Nola was probably right, given that Grayson had reacted to the name "Anna" and not the girl's name. Eric wanted to volunteer this information but doubted it would make much difference.

Jack Dalton considered Nola's words. "Regardless, the police should handle this, Nola. Grayson may be involved. He may be trying to get you involved. I know you're not going to want to hear this, but you should stay out of this."

"Didn't I already tell you I was through working with the PD? I do my own thing these days, Jack."

Eric was so focused on the complex cacophony of vibes, he almost missed Nola getting up and heading out the door. He stumbled out of his chair after her, glancing at Jack Dalton to mutter good-bye. Dalton ignored him.

Screw you, Eric thought, shuffling to keep up with Nola. But there was one thing he himself could not ignore: the last vibes he'd gotten from Dalton were uneasy ones.

4

"WELL, THAT EXPLAINS WHY he called me out of the blue."

They were back in the car. Nola put the key in the ignition but didn't turn it just yet. At first Eric wondered if she was talking about Dalton, but then realized it must have been that man—Grayson, the one waiting outside the apartment. "He, um, called you? That guy I saw? What'd he want?"

She nodded absently, staring at the dashboard. "Yes, he called earlier today. I didn't take the call. Haven't even checked the voice mail message yet." She turned to him with a wry half-smile. "That's just how it is, you know?"

Eric had no clue. He gave her a clueless-sounding "uh huh."

"Well. I suppose I ought to get you back to your mother." She started the car. Eric hoped she hadn't noticed him wince; the reference to his mother somehow made it sound like she was his nanny and he a small child. They were in all likelihood close to the same age, but Nola somehow seemed so self-possessed and assured, qualities Eric lacked. Even when he played poker, he didn't act confident so much as blank. He could read them better than they could read him, but that didn't always mean he was a better player.

Right now he felt like a player in a game in which he didn't know the rules and wasn't even sure what the game was. He spoke before he could stop himself. "Are you going to go see him?"

She glanced at him, surprised. "Grayson? Yeah, guess I might as well find out what the deal is."

He gambled. "Would you feel better if someone was there with you?"

Now she smiled. "You know, actually, I would. But if you mean you, that's not necessary. Thanks, seriously, but there's no need for you to get involved in this, and I'm sure your mom wants to see you."

"She's going to see plenty of me all week," he said quickly, then realized how callous that might sound. "I don't mind. And actually I kind of want to, I don't know, explain to that guy. Why I acted so weird. Since I guess that's the only reason he followed me." Of course, he couldn't really explain, could he? "Or at least sort of try to clear up the thing that happened on the train. In case I bump into him again, and he thinks I'm the one following him."

He was pleased with his reasoning, even though it was highly unlikely that he'd "bump into" someone like Grayson Bryant. Redfort wasn't a big town, but rich and poor were sharply segregated and seldom had contact. It wasn't hard to figure out what side of town Bryant was from based on the expensive car and suit.

She hesitated, but nothing in her vibes suggested she opposed the idea. "Tell you what. I'm hungry. You must be, too. Let's pull into Martinelli's. I'll call him—Grayson—and see what he wants. I doubt he's still waiting outside the apartment. If he wants to talk to me in person he can meet us for a slice."

For a moment Eric relished the idea of the man in the expensive clothes dealing with greasy triangles of pizza. The guy had probably never set foot in Martinelli's in his life. Then it occurred to him that he himself hadn't set foot in the place since high school, a time he'd tried to forget. At least this time he had a pretty girl with him instead of—well, no one. He wondered how long he'd get to be with the pretty girl before Mr. Expensive Suit appeared and claimed Nola's attention the way Jack Dalton had—the way, her vibes told him, he himself failed to do.

OF COURSE HE SHOWED up only minutes after Nola called. Of course he knew Gary Martinelli personally—helped finance his restaurants, it seemed—and a bottle of Chianti from the owner's private stock soon appeared at their table. Of course he was suave and sophisticated, Act II to ruggedly handsome Jack. Eric felt tension in Nola's vibes, a tension that could suggest anything from mistrust to unwilling attraction—and probably a little of each.

"Grayson," she said stiffly and then gestured with unnecessary vigor at Eric—a gesture, Eric guessed, given the tension, meant to keep Grayson at arm's length. "This is Eric Lafferty, my neighbor's son."

When the man finally turned his attention from Nola (just barely—he fairly screamed libidinous vibes), there was only the barest blip of recognition of Eric followed by faint puzzlement, nothing more. He wasn't alarmed or defensive; he acted like a person who'd met someone vaguely familiar whom he couldn't quite place. He shook Eric's hand firmly and nodded his head.

Nola was watching both of them, and was clearly just as puzzled. Eric had made a big deal about something that seemed not to have fazed Grayson. The business on the train appeared to have been a coincidence or a simple misunderstanding. As someone who read vibes, however, Eric believed things were never quite as they appeared on the surface.

Grayson, Eric was informed, was a sports doctor. Of course. And what did Eric do? Wait tables at chain restaurants in between poker games, basically. At first his "day job" had seemed like a bad idea given the cacophony of vibes around him, but he soon found it to be a good way to get more practice reading them. When he approached a table where people were having a tense conversation, he knew enough to steer clear and come back later. When a patron took one bite of his meal and his vibes went kablooey, Eric turned immediately and asked if everything was OK. He got good tips, useful cash for after his shift finished and he headed to the next game. He didn't say any of this to Grayson and Nola, though. He just said "waiter."

"Eric is here for his father's funeral," Nola said.

It seemed like a socially awkward thing to say, but Eric read determination from her and figured she'd said it to justify his presence. It still made no sense, but then Grayson might not want to be rude to someone who was supposedly mourning. Nola clearly did not want to be alone with Grayson. Eric had no intention of letting that happen.

"I need to talk to you. It's about Anna." A faint smile appeared on Grayson's face. "But then you knew that already, didn't you. I suppose you've been questioned by the White Knight?"

"Of course Jack Dalton asked me if I had any relevant information. I know Anna and I'm running her store. Naturally he—"

"Dalton's got it all wrong," Grayson said, adding, "Now there's a shocker. Anna had nothing to do with the thrill kill group despite what the latest news leak is saying. Her connection to the Lasky girl was of a very different nature."

"She tell you this or is this your own theory?"

Grayson took a sip of wine, his eyes never leaving hers. Eric gnawed the crust of his slice. It tasted like cardboard. "I saw her three days ago." Grayson put the wine down before speaking again. His sense of drama was different from Jack Dalton's—more calculated—but just as annoying to Eric. "She came to see me about something unrelated to this matter, but she also mentioned a few relevant details. She wasn't all that forthcoming, but it had to do with this group she's in."

Eric blurted, "I thought you said she had nothing to do with—"

"It's an entirely different type of group," Grayson interrupted without even looking at Eric. "They consider themselves Wiccan, or at least a vaguely related sect thereof. They go to places where people died painful deaths and perform rituals to honor the dead. They got Anna involved a couple months ago because they believe trace is the part of the soul still lingering—still suffering. They exorcise that 'soul.'"

"Meaning . . . they expected Anna to remove the trace. Did she?" asked Nola.

Grayson gave her a frosty smile. "Which would be worse, do you suppose, pretending to take the trace or really taking it?"

Nola returned his look without the smile.

"In any case, here's what Anna told me. She said this group had been going on for a few months. There are about a dozen or so members, though only a small number of 'regulars' participated every week. Each week someone picked a place to perform their ritual. Sometimes the place had a personal connection to one of the members, but other times it was just something they'd read about in the news. Three weeks ago they went to the place where one of those homeless men had been killed. They did that because Sabrina Lasky had just joined the group."

Grayson poured more wine for Nola before continuing. "She claimed the man had been her uncle, but Anna thought the girl's reaction was much stronger than you'd expect even for very close extended family—'crying her eyes out,' as she put it. After Lasky's death, Anna figured it out."

Nola sat still, her vibes intently focused. Eric was dying to snap her out of it and warn her not to get involved, but he didn't dare. Finally, she spoke. "The timing of all this is very troubling. Lasky appears in the group claiming to be related to one of the thrill kill victims. She disappears shortly thereafter. Then her body turns up in an alley in a seedy part of town. Apparently she jumped or was pushed from an upper floor of one of the surrounding buildings.

"Two possibilities. First, the thrill-kill group thought she was going to rat them out, so one of them found her and killed her. That, I'm guessing, is what the police believe. Or—someone else in the group figured out Lasky's real connection to the dead man and blackmailed or otherwise threatened her to the point of suicide."

Grayson, annoyingly, was smiling again. "So you agree that the police are wrong about Anna's involvement?"

If vibes could be described as "smirky," this man's would qualify.

"I believe they don't have enough information at present—information which you could have supplied to them. Don't bother, Grayson." She held up her hand before Grayson could open his mouth. "I know you refuse to play nice with the police—even though Anna is involved."

"Anna is not involved. Isn't that just what I got through explaining?"

"Anna is missing, Grayson. Don't you find that timing a little suspicious as well? What if whoever killed Lasky thought Anna might also know something?"

"Anna's disappearance has nothing to do with this matter."

"What were you doing downstate?"

The question surprised both men. That, Eric realized, had been intentional, at least as far as Grayson was concerned. Nola Lantri knew how to interrogate a suspect—assuming Grayson was still a suspect. Eric sure thought of him as one.

"Anna has distant family on Long Island. I went to see if she might be there. She isn't. I don't know where she is."

Grayson said nothing more, just kept steady eye contact with Nola. The man's vibes gave nothing away. He didn't seem to be lying, but something else was going on with him. Eric had no idea what it could be, but he didn't like it regardless.

"Grayson." The slight shift in Nola's vibes made Eric lean forward even more, as though that would help him figure out what was going on in her head. "I am as concerned as you are about Anna. But why are you telling me all of this, especially since you won't give me any information?"

Grayson stared for an uncomfortably long time at Nola—uncomfortable for Eric, at least, since neither of the other two seemed vibe-bothered by it. "Anna called you when she wanted something done, not me. I suppose I'm just honoring what I believe to be her wishes."

"Something done? She wanted me to ring up sales of organic oatmeal. What does that have to do with ..." Nola's vibes lurched. She turned toward Eric, for no particular reason except perhaps to include him, finally, in the conversation. "Wait a minute. There was a group of people."

Eric remembered what she'd said: four people, right at closing time. "You think that was the Wiccan group, or whatever they're called?" he asked. She nodded. "Could one of them have been responsible for Sabrina Lasky's death if they figured out who she was?"

Grayson swiftly reentered the conversation. "What did you say to the group?"

"I just told them to come back tomorrow. I thought there was a chance maybe she'd be back by then, since she never really gave me an end date."

"She won't be back then." He didn't give an explanation, and Nola didn't ask for one.

"Well, I guess I can go back there tomorrow evening. Meet with the group. See what I can find out. It can't hurt, and maybe it could help clear Anna's name if I can report back to Ja… to the police that her group is not involved with the thrill killers." She locked eyes with Grayson, vibes bold, and added, "I still don't see why Anna would want my help like this."

"Because she trusts you. She didn't ask for my help because she doesn't trust me."

I don't trust you either, thought Eric. If Nola's thumping vibes beneath her cool exterior were any indication, neither did she.

"I'M SO SORRY YOU had to get involved in all of this, but luckily you can consider your involvement completed. As they say, in some very unrelated situation, 'I'll take it from here.'"

They were back at the apartment. Their respective doors loomed ahead at the end of the hallway, and Eric suddenly felt panicky. "Don't you think the cops should take care of this?" He hated to push her back toward Jack Dalton but didn't see a better alternative. "I mean, there's been a murder. This all seems pretty dangerous."

She grinned. "Well, you know how dull Redfort is. I could use a little dangerousness. It's that or another trip to the mall, and nothing's on sale right now." She laughed as he continued to stare at her. "I'll be careful, I promise. I'm just trying to get some information, not take down some bad guys. What terrible calamity could possibly befall me when I'm surrounded by all that hippy-dippy happiness in Anna's store?"

"Would you be doing this if Grayson hadn't been the one to ask?"

Eric didn't need to get her vibes to know the question surprised her. It surprised him. Why the hell had that come out of his mouth? *Because it's what you were thinking.* Unwillingly he met her eyes. She seemed to be wavering between two emotions, two out-of-sync of pulses in competition. Her voice had its usual steady coolness when she finally answered. "I am doing this for Anna. Not for Grayson, and not for Jack. She asked me for help. I'm going to help." She turned away and walked briskly toward her own apartment door. "Give my regards to your mother," she added and then shut her door behind her.

5

"How was the train ride? Have you eaten anything? Did you like Nola?"

Eric stared. The third question caught his attention, since he was still thinking about Nola as he greeted his mother. And he was supposed to be the one who could read minds. "Train was fine. Ate at Martinelli's." He didn't supply a third answer. He knew his mother wouldn't press him for one. During his teen years his mother had gotten used to the fact that Eric only spoke when he absolutely had to, to the point where she wasn't bothered that most of what she said to him went without response. It wasn't that he didn't listen. He did. She knew this, too.

"That's good. Nola has been such a big help to me these last few days," his mother continued as though he actually had answered the final query. "There's been so much to do, you know. Sometimes it's just overwhelming!" She laughed and put an affectionate hand on his shoulder. "I'm so glad you made it back."

Eric nodded absently. He was still trying to take in all he saw. He'd expected the apartment to be a gloomy mess. He was shocked to find it not just clean and organized but beautiful. His mother had clearly vacuumed and dusted and polished; she'd even put the condolence bouquets in vases around the living room so that they seemed like part of the décor and not simply garish splotches of color.

His mother rushed over to the coffee table, where she had been trimming flowers to put in a white porcelain bowl. "Ikebana," she said as though apologizing. "Japanese flower arranging? I just started a class. These are the wrong kinds of flowers, I'm sure, but it's good practice, and it puts them to good use. It's funny, people sending these. James hated flowers." She laughed again. Eric knew from her vibes that it wasn't the nervous, strained laughter of someone under stress. She was calm, relaxed. She looked older, of course, with more grey in her hair, more wrinkles around her eyes, though no more than one would expect. She was 60 and looked it, but the years had not worn her away before her time. Still he stared at her as though it had been a hundred years since he'd seen her and not just under ten.

Eric had no connection to this place, had never been there before; his parents had sold their old house years ago. His mother had claimed it was "too big for just the two of them," but Eric knew the real reason. She was afraid his father would fall down the stairs in a drunken stupor and break his neck. Eric had no idea what the apartment looked like when his father was there, and now he would never know that because this place seemed all Angela Lafferty. She'd taken care of her husband through the end of his life. Now she was getting on with hers.

Instead of feeling comforted by her strength, he felt a sudden surge of anger. Why hadn't she shown this kind of life and energy in the past? Why did she let herself—and him—be bossed around by that bastard? He threw himself on the sofa, feeling like he'd just turned the clock back and become a sullen seventeen again.

"I think Nola is the same age as you." She fussed with the flowers. "Do you remember her from school at all?"

"She probably went to Sterling," Eric said, staring at the oddly angled stems. There were two local high schools, Sterling and Royal, one at each end of the valley. Despite the lofty sounding names, both consisted of identical ugly brown buildings and identically dressed students. The Sterling kids called Eric's school "Royal Pita," the "pita" meaning "pain in the ass." When the schools' football teams played each other in the Big Game, the Sterling side waved pita bread at the Royal side. Privately Eric called it Royal Pita himself. He'd hated his years there.

"Well, in any case, I hope you get to spend some time with her while you're here. She works over at the courts normally but she witnessed a shooting last week at close range—can you believe?—and her boss pretty much forced her to take paid medical leave for the trauma."

"I know. She told me. She said she hates it because it makes her sound crazy."

"Oh, did she say that?" She turned to face him, her smile now slightly mischievous, and he realized this was the most he'd spoken since he got there. "She must like you if she told you all that." She met his gaze, smile fading, put down her scissors and leaned back on the sofa next to him. Something changed in her vibe, but he wasn't sure what it meant. "Eric," she said quietly. "I know how hard this is for you."

He bolted up from the sofa and stepped away from her. "No," he blurted, answering something she hadn't asked.

His mother looked down at her hands. "Eric, everyone needs help sometimes. If you're the one in need, and you get that help, hopefully you'll remember it, and you'll be there for someone else when they need help too. That's why I stuck with your father. I don't expect you to understand, and I'm not saying you should have stayed. I'm proud of you. I'm glad you have your own life now."

It occurred to him to say he was glad she had one now too, but he couldn't. He was seventeen again, angry and confused. She looked up at him and smiled anyway, as though she understood.

ALTHOUGH EVERYTHING SEEMED PRETTY much in order, Angela Lafferty insisted that there was still so much to be done and she was glad Eric was there because she simply couldn't manage without him. His first order of business the next morning was to try to sell his father's car. They should have sold it earlier instead of paying for the extra parking space, as well as insurance and other costs, since his father was always too wasted to drive. Eric couldn't fathom why they'd hung on to it.

He drank his coffee in silence. It was already 10:30; he wasn't used to getting up early and had forgotten about the time change. As he heard without registering his mother's list of breakfast options—"bagels, bananas, blueberry muffins, and at least a couple of things that don't start with the letter 'B'"—he thought about taking the car to Albany, where he'd get a better price for it, and perhaps swing by the store where Nola was going and see if she wanted to have lunch. Of course, if he did sell the car he'd have to take the bus home—unless he could get a ride from Nola. That would be a bit of an imposition, and a bit strange, too. Of course, if she didn't already think he was strange after yesterday, this wouldn't likely change anything. It was most likely a big stupid waste of time. But what else did he have to do? He certainly didn't have to stay home and look after his mother. She had her own list of things to do and was ready to launch into them. Who knows, he thought, draining his cup, perhaps flower arranging would be followed by karate. He wouldn't put it past her.

Yet despite her outward cheer something in her vibes sounded low and heavy and hushed, as though it came from underwater. He'd never heard it before—or perhaps he hadn't been listening closely enough. As she handed him the car keys, pressing them in his hands, her touch lingering ever so slightly—keys she'd frequently hid from her husband despite every vicious, vile thing he screamed at her so he wouldn't drive while stinking drunk—he wondered if, in spite of everything, this was grief.

ERIC HAD NEVER GRIEVED for anyone, but he'd tasted plenty of life's disappointment. He was tasting it right now as he sat in his car watching Nola and Grayson leave the Natural Living store and make their way over to the little Indian restaurant down the block. Bombay Bistro. He wondered if they served their vindaloo on croissants. He leaned forward and thudded his forehead against the steering wheel. What an idiot he was, thinking he could just cruise on over to Albany and whisk her away to lunch. He'd met her yesterday. She and Grayson clearly had a history. And anyway, what the hell made Eric think he could have any part in her life? They might be the same age, but Nola seemed leaps and bounds ahead of him in maturity and just the general state of having one's shit together.

He sat up again. There was no point in hanging around here. He hardly wanted to sit inertly until they came back and spotted him and wondered why the hell he was waiting there all stalkerish and creepy. Yet he hesitated to put the key in the ignition. What was he doing here, anyway? Not here, Albany, but here, at this point in his life. He hadn't been back 24 hours and he was already chasing after something pointless—like he had been all those years, trying to understand vibes, only to come to the realization that knowing what people were thinking gave you no insights whatsoever as to why they were thinking it or how they might act on those thoughts. Despite knowing something other people did not, he felt he understood less rather than more about the world around him.

An anxious looking young man approached the Natural Living store. He was probably a university student, undergraduate age with the appropriate grunge look. He frowned at the "Back at 1" sign, tried the door anyway, then cupped his hands to the glass and peered inside. Dude's just got to have his flaxseed oil, Eric thought humorlessly.

The boy did not leave. Instead he kept peering into windows and tapping them urgently. What in the world did he want? The faint vibes Eric got were aggressive, yet they were not well controlled. He couldn't be planning to rob the store—and anyway, who would do that in the middle of the day? Besides, the store could hardly have much cash lying around or anything lucrative to resell. The boy had to be searching for Anna. When he didn't find her, surely he would leave.

The boy came around the side of the store where Eric's car was parked, and Eric instinctively hunched down. On the other hand, he thought, feeling ridiculous as well as cowardly, he might just be a common everyday criminal. At closer range Eric could see this was no college student affect-ing a grunge look. The boy looked like he'd been in a few fights rather than football games. His pacing had an animal sort of energy, as did his vibes. Still, what could Eric do? Without a phone, he couldn't call 911, and he'd be damned if he would scurry down the street to tell Nola—and The Sports Doctor—that someone was skulking around the store in a suspicious fashion and then leave them to deal with it.

The boy came back to the front of the store and glanced around several times. Eric stayed hunched down, straining to see over the dashboard. He had a strong feeling he knew what was about to happen. Sure enough, the boy pulled something from the pocket of his jeans and began to pick the lock. It took him seconds to open it.

Eric had never been good at reading vibes connected to sudden instinct. They went too fast to register—whether the instinct was someone else's or his own. He jumped out of the car and ran to the now open door, before his conscious mind could wonder what the hell he was doing or why. He just moved. "Are you looking for someone?"

The boy froze in the doorway without turning around. Eric remained outside the store where he could be seen from the street, though he was standing close enough that the boy could easily do some damage with fist or weapon. The boy craned his head. "Anna. I'm looking for Anna." He turned slowly to face Eric. "You know her?"

"Sort of. Not really. I mean, I'm a friend of a friend of hers."

The boy's expression did not change. "You know where she is?"

"No. I really don't. She's kind of missing. I—we, my friend and I—were hoping to find her ourselves."

"Missing?" The boy's voice cracked on the word, and he backed into the store shaking his head as though he'd received some unfathomably bad news. "Missing? No. Oh, fuck no. I got to find her."

Eric didn't like that the boy was moving further into the store. Although he didn't like not being visible to the street traffic, he entered the store himself, keeping close to the doorway, holding the door open with his foot. "What are you . . . why are you looking for her?"

The boy looked desperately around the room as though Anna might still be there somehow. "I got to find her."

"Well, she's not here, so why don't we get out of here and—"

"And what?" the boy spat. His vibes were pounding, but once again it was anxiety, not aggression. "You gonna call the cops?"

"No, but you are kind of breaking and entering, you know." Hastily, Eric added, "Look, I'm not going to call the cops. I'm just saying I need to know why you're here."

"I told you. I'm looking for Anna. I got to find her."

Eric took a chance. "Is this about Sabrina Lasky?"

For a moment he thought he'd made the biggest mistake of his soon-to-be-short life. The boy's vibes thundered. His body froze and his voice became as thin and cold as a steel blade. "The fuck do you know about that?"

"Nothing. They were friends, Anna and Sabrina. That's all I know. I don't know what happened to either of them." That wasn't quite right; he did know what happened to Sabrina, he just didn't know how.

"Sabrina's dead. Dead." Suddenly the boy closed his eyes, his posture going slack. His raging vibes now rang hollowly through the space between them. He opened his eyes and stared at the floor. "The cops think I did it. Brought me in for questioning. Fuckers. I didn't kill her. I loved her. She loved me."

All the more reason for them to think you killed her, Eric thought but didn't dare say. "Do you think Anna knows who did it?"

He nodded, eyes still downcast. "Brina trusted her. She told me—" Suddenly his eyes snapped up and locked on Eric's. "Hey. Who the fuck are you anyway."

"I said, I'm a friend of a friend of—"

"Yeah, friend of a friend of a friend of fuck all," he snarled. "Look, friend. All I know is Brina told me to trust this woman Anna. She didn't say nothing about trusting you. You tell me where Anna is or get the fuck out of my way now."

The boy pulled out a knife.

6

"**P**UT THAT DOWN."

Nola stood at the door. She spoke calmly but firmly to the boy with the knife, as though she dealt with these kinds of situations every day. She was alone—no Grayson Bryant at her side.

His eyes darted from Eric to Nola, then back to Nola. "You Anna?"

"I'm Anna's friend, Nola. I'm taking care of her business while she's away."

"Where is she?"

"Anna isn't here. I don't know where she is and I can't contact her. Please. Put the knife down so we can talk."

He hesitated, but Eric knew he was backing down, vibes calming with the sound of her voice. Nola's vibes remained cool as a gently rippling pond.

The boy put the knife away. "Sorry. Shouldn't have done that."

"What's your name?" Nola asked. "How do you know Anna?"

"Max. I don't know Anna. I got to find her though. She knows who killed my girlfriend."

"Sabrina Lasky," Eric said, annoyed at how croaky-nervous he still sounded.

Nola walked slowly into the store, keeping her eyes on Max after one fleeting glance at Eric, which made Eric realize his own appearance in the store was just as strange as the boy's. "I came to Albany for some, um, business stuff. For my mother. I happened to be passing by and saw him," he nodded at Max, "breaking into the store."

"I wasn't gonna steal nothing," Max snarled at Eric. He turned back to Nola, his voice softened. "The cops think I killed Brina. I got to find out who did. Last I talked to Brina, she said she met this woman, Anna, who was helping her. She said she trusted Anna. Said Anna was a good person."

"She is a good person, but she isn't here. Maybe we can help you, though. Why don't you tell me what you know?"

The boy stared at her for an uncomfortably long time, but there was nothing alarming in his vibes. Just as Sabrina had trusted Anna, Eric had the feeling Max would trust Nola. He marveled at this: How did they know? How did this boy look at Nola and decide, yes, she was OK? If other people couldn't read vibes, on what could they base their decisions? But maybe they were better off that way, going with some vague "gut instinct" that didn't have to be understood or explained, just blindly followed.

Max leaned toward Nola and began to speak, his voice subdued. "Brina was hanging out with some . . . friends of mine. She didn't like some of the shit that was going down with them after a while, so a couple weeks ago she took off. I thought maybe she went back home—the city—but she didn't. I been looking for her. I called her a billion times to get her back. Finally she answered. Told me she'd 'made peace' with all that stuff in the past and she was ready to see me, but she wasn't going back with the group anymore. I said fine. I just wanted to see her. I really did. I didn't care about nothing else.

"The last person she saw—last person who didn't kill her—was Anna. The last person she talked to was me. When she answered my call, she told me she'd just been talking to this friend of hers. That was Anna, and they were here. Brina said she was going back to the place she was staying—this place out by the warehouse district—and told me meet her there.

"One more thing she said I remember: she thought someone was following her when she left Anna. She thought at first it was me, then maybe one of the boys—my friends. I said it wasn't me and it couldn't have been one of them; they didn't know where she was or where I was.

"So I went to where she told me, but it was too late. The cops were all over the place. I didn't even get to see her. They'd already taken her—her body—away."

Eric felt the change in vibes a beat before Max's voice turned steel-hard and cold. "Next thing I know they're bringing me in for questioning. Said people saw me in the area where she'd been killed. Of course the fuckers saw me. I was there—after. But dumbasses get an idea put in their head and they forget whether it's after or before, all they know is some freaky-looking guy was there and yeah, he must be the one."

Max was right—it was so easy for the police to manipulate witnesses into thinking they'd seen a suspect at a certain time and place when no such thing had ever happened. There were reasons for the police to suspect Max even if no one had claimed to see him at the scene of the crime, but Eric knew before she'd said a word that Nola was starting to believe him.

"I am sorry, Max. I don't know much about this—Anna didn't tell me anything—but ..." Nola paused to lean forward, speaking and vibing as though she and Max were the only two people in the room, "I will try to help you."

As SOON AS MAX left, Nola asked, "What are you doing here?" Her tone didn't require a reading of vibes to understand. She was irritated.

"I told you, I had business to do here. I mean, I'm selling my father's car."

"What, nobody buys cars in Redfort? Anyway, that's not what I meant. I meant what are you doing *here*? While this place sells stuff on consignment, a car doesn't quite fit, you know?"

Eric had won thousands of dollars in a game that was essentially all about lying, but now his brain froze and he couldn't make up a story about knowing someone in this general neighborhood who was interested in the old Ford. "I came by to see if you wanted to have lunch. But you'd already gone." He gestured unnecessarily at the "Back at 1" sign. "Saw that guy—Max—breaking in, and—"

"You couldn't have called the cops?"

"I don't have a phone."

She sighed, whether in disdain or resignation or something else Eric was too mired in embarrassment to figure out. "Well, good thing I got back well before one, I guess."

"Yeah—I thought you were having lunch there."

"Having lunch where?" Her vibes sparked in confused interest and Eric wished he'd kept his mouth shut.

"Wherever. I mean, wherever you were going."

She stared at him another uncomfortable moment. "I got it to go." She held up a white plastic bag that appeared to be holding a couple of take-out clamshell boxes. As if on cue, Eric noticed the strong aroma of spicy curry sauce. She must have sent Grayson on his way for some reason. Eric shook his head involuntarily. His father used to say a parade of elephants could march through the living room, followed by a brass band and a tank, and Eric would miss all of it.

Nola walked briskly to the back of the store. "Well, since you're here and neither of us have eaten, you might as well join me." She began unpacking the bag on the table that held coffee and tea makers for customers to try free samples.

"I wouldn't want to take away any of your food," he mumbled.

"You wouldn't be depriving me. In fact, you might be doing me a favor because these portions are ridiculous. One box is full of garlic naan and rice, and the other has a vegetable curry and a lamb curry, and I think they've thrown in a couple of fritter-type items somewhere as well."

There was indeed an enormous amount of food, all of it fragrant and spicy and, Eric discovered after a few bites, delicious. They ate in silence for a while. He was dying to ask what happened to Grayson, but he couldn't bring it up without revealing that he'd seen them together. Anyway, he knew it was none of his business. He'd been prying into Nola's affairs too much already.

"So what do you think of this whole business with Max and Sabrina and Anna?" Nola said, reaching for a pakora.

Eric chewed his curry extra thoroughly before swallowing. "I think the whole business is none of my business. And considering there's a murder and a lot of other bad stuff going on, it probably shouldn't be yours either, frankly."

"It is my business," Nola said as though she'd been anticipating his words. "Anna asked for my help. I know, I know, she just wanted my help in watching the store, but she could have chosen anyone to do that. She has part-time cashiers for weekends and busy seasons; she could have asked one of those people if she just wanted someone to ring up purchases and stuff. Anyone else would be better at that than I am since I don't know half the stuff in here. She chose me because she knows the work I've done and she wanted someone who might figure out what happened—if something happened, which it has."

"But what happened? It could be anything."

"Think about it. Anna is missing. Nobody knows where she is. If she knew who killed Sabrina, that could explain her absence. Either she's trying to get away from that person, or . . . well . . . "

"They got her," Eric said flatly.

"Yeah," Nola said, echoing his tone. "Maybe they did. Either way I owe it to her to find out."

"Let me help. If you insist on getting involved, I can help."

"No thanks. Anna asked me to be here, no one else. I don't need anyone else in on this, not Grayson, not Jack, not you."

Perhaps this explained why Nola sent Grayson away without the satisfaction of her company at lunch: he had tried to get involved. "Those people in the group are coming back again this afternoon, right?" he argued. "If you talk about the murder and one of them knows something, I would be able to tell. If one of them shows a vibe reaction far stronger than the others, that's a pretty good sign." Of course, they wouldn't know what it was a sign of, exactly—after all, he'd gotten strong vibes from Grayson and completely misread them. "We'd have a place to start, anyway."

Nola put down her fork and stared thoughtfully at the bits of rice and vegetables left on her plate. *He has a point*—Eric could almost hear the words rippling from her mind. She looked up at him. "Why exactly are you doing this?"

Good question. It was like he'd been forcing himself on her the minute they met, pushing himself into her life like a stalker. He shrugged. "Guess I'm trying to avoid the real reason I came back."

She smiled faintly. "You think?"

That made him laugh. "Just a hunch, based on my superhero instincts."

He knew that wasn't the only reason. He knew that despite his difference, despite his freak-show ability, he wanted what everyone wanted: a meaningful life. When his father died, it was as though curtains partially drawn across a window had been flung open. Only thing was he had no idea what exactly he was seeing out that window—or whether he even wanted to see it.

To keep her from asking more questions he wasn't ready to answer, he asked one of her. "Why didn't you ever leave Redfort?"

As soon as he said it, he realized how it might sound—as though he were sneering at her for being one of those townies who never left their own zip code. Nola took it in stride, though, a half-smile playing on her lips. "I thought about leaving all the time. Still do. New York City is a bus ride away, and I've had sufficient fare money for ten years now." She shrugged. "I could use the tracism as an excuse. Cities are full of the dead, you know."

He nodded; he hadn't thought of that. But then she waved the idea aside. "That would be a lie, though. I guess at some point I figured it doesn't much matter where you are when you're unhappy. A place isn't going to change anything. If you're unhappy in the place that helped form the person you are, you're probably more unhappy with yourself than the place." The half-smile became a full one. "Oooooooh, deep, huh. And now that I've said that, why did you decide not to stay?"

"Because I didn't figure that out."

She laughed. He liked the sound, liked the feel of her vibes along with the sound.

Nola picked up her fork again and pointed it at him emphatically. "OK, you're in. Do what you have to do this afternoon with your dad's car and be back at 4 p.m. We'll go over our strategy for dealing with these people before they get here. And take the trash with you, please. Most of the customers here are vegan. They'll run screaming when they find out we've been eating baby sheep."

7

THE USED-CAR DEALER WAS nothing like his stereotype. Eric had expected some sleazy guy who called him "sport" or "champ" or "pal," smiled too toothily with too-gleaming eyes while he tried to bilk Eric for every last cent he could. Instead he got a mild-mannered, middle-aged man who gave off not one disconcerting vibe the whole time Eric was there. Eric got the price he wanted, without any sense that he'd asked too little and the guy would chortle about it to his buddies later.

The dealer gave him a ride back to the general vicinity of Natural Living, not right to it. Eric didn't want to be early and seem overly eager, so he hung around the used bookstores and second-hand clothing shops for an hour and a half. He was older than most of the other hangers-around, but he didn't seem out of place. Everyone around him had an aimlessness, their vibes like shallow pulses. Barely alive—was that his own existence?

Eric slid men's suits on their hangers from one end of the rack to the other, barely registering what they looked like, even when they were hard to ignore—turquoise with wide lapels, pinstripes that went diagonally. He wanted a meaningful life. He thought he could make one, yet he'd felt held back until now. He could blame his father, but really, did that even make sense? He thought about what Nola had said about why she'd never left Redfort: It doesn't much matter where you are when you're unhappy. A place isn't going to change anything . . . you're probably more unhappy with yourself than the place. By extension, it wasn't Redfort or his unhappy childhood in Redfort or his bad relationship with his father. He was responsible for his life, for making it meaningful—or failing to do so.

He glanced at his watch. It was nearly time to return to the store. He wanted to make good on his offer of help. Yes, he wanted to impress Nola, but there had to be more to it. He turned from the rack of clothes and strode out onto the street, determined to make whatever happened the "more to it" he sought.

Of course, slowing his approach as he neared the shop door, sensing a cloud of vibes ahead, he wasn't sure how to do that.

❖

ONE NEW SET OF vibes he could deal with. Large crowds he could tune out. Small groups were the worst. When he played poker he could handle it because he only had to interact with the others in very limited ways. But when he was expected to introduce himself, and hear their introductions, and converse with them in a socially acceptable way—it was the stuff of nightmares. You're just shy, people would say. You can get over it. Not only did he find that insulting advice by itself—always given by people who had no idea what "shy" meant—but it was also wrong. He wasn't shy. He was hearing two different voices at once. It was as though every time he met someone, he was meeting two people speaking two different languages at the same time. Which should he focus on? It didn't matter; he couldn't focus on just one. He tried to listen to their words, but their vibes always got his attention first.

In poker, a player could take only so many actions, so it was a lot easier for him to make use of input from them. In his job, people's reactions were fairly limited and predictable as well. In the rest of the world, however, the metaphoric deck contained nearly an infinite number of cards. He could find a change in the pattern, but he didn't know what the change meant.

There were six people in the room including Nola and himself. To learn anything useful, he had to get used to the patterns of their thoughts before he could know when they changed. And right now they were all upset in general and uneasy with his presence in particular.

In other words, this was going to be tough.

Six people in a room, five sets of vibes crashing through his head. He could barely look at these people, register their features, guess their ages, remember their names, because the vibes commanded all his focus. Was the woman with the bright-red hair reacting to what the person next to her was saying, or was she staring at Eric and reacting to him? Was the older woman next to the redhead telling a lie, or did her vibes always sound that way? Was the plump, owlish woman of indeterminate age excited, agitated, or ill? Was the silent middle-aged man next to Eric even listening to anyone in the room at all?

Can't believe . . . ever found out about . . . not sure why they . . . for about four years . . . don't think she should have said anything about . . . that's just not right, I mean, because . . . downtown . . . falling . . . six months ago they . . . awful . . . is it . . . what do you . . .

Eric suddenly realized the voices had stopped. They were all looking at him; apparently someone (Nola?) had addressed him and expected him to respond.

He had no idea how to respond.

"Again, I know this is a lot of new stuff happening," Nola said, clearly repeating what she'd just said for his benefit. "But I am fully able to perform Anna's duties to this group. And our new member is fully aware of this group's mission." She turned pointedly back to him, and it didn't take any special powers for Eric to know this was his cue. "Why don't you introduce yourself?"

"Um, yeah. I'm Eric. From Redfort."

"Well, Eric from Redfort," said the older woman of the group with a smile. She had silver hair, silver jewelry, and vibes that gave him no alarm, at least at the moment. "Welcome. Why did you decide to join us?"

(Vibes light, tinkly, like silver, though with the coldness of silver too, like a shiver.)

He should have been ready for that question—of course someone was bound to ask it. Why hadn't he thought up a good story? Before he could answer, the redheaded woman with the astonishing number of facial piercings squawked—there could be no other word for the sound of her voice—"Yeah, Eric from Redfort, why join us ghouls?"

(Vibes like the activity in a diner kitchen—clanging and crashing, but also purposeful, with its own sort of rhythm.)

"Oh really, now. Ghouls!" the silvery woman protested.

"That's what they call us. Because of our 'obsession' with the dead. That's how they always put it," the pierced woman said, and Eric had the sense she was including him with they.

"Nonsense!" This suddenly from the middle-aged man, who until that point had said nothing. His suit looked like it had come from the thrift shop, and there were paint stains on his hands. "There is no 'they' talking about us. I do not care about 'they.' I care about us, this group, this ghoulish death-obsessed group. And I would like to know, as would we all, why you wish to join us."

(Vibes that seemed to wind and curl like Baroque music, complex, coiled, mysterious.)

"My father," Eric blurted. Everyone stared at him, including Nola. "My father died recently. He . . . suffered a lot, and he made people suffer a lot, and I want to, to, alleviate some of that suffering."

No one spoke, no one's vibes gave anything away.

The last of the four, the plump owlish woman who had not addressed him yet, placed her hand gently on his forearm. "Ah. We understand."

(Vibes that reminded him of . . . something. They were soothing, at least, and relatively calm.)

Relief flooded him. He'd passed the test. If they'd been able to read his own vibes, they'd probably wonder about his agitation. Nola, who likely already knew of his agitation, smoothly took over.

"Thanks, Eric. Well, according to Anna we're supposed to pick the next place and date." The four nodded. "As I understand it, we always give any new members the chance to pick a personal location first if they need to." She turned again to Eric, her face a controlled blank.

He paused, not to build suspense (they couldn't know that what he was going to say would be suspenseful), but to get as solid a fix on their vibes as he could. "The Biltmore. Where Sabrina Lasky died."

The easiest thing to read in a group of people was aberration. Which one of these things was not like the other? Everyone was shocked, of course, but one person was very shocked—and remained so, after everyone else's vibes had eased. One person's vibes jackhammered at him until he could barely keep from running out of the room to escape.

It came from one of them. He just wasn't sure which one. He was sure, however, that whoever had that violent reaction, it was directed toward him. He did not even know their names, but he knew—he knew—that one of them wanted to kill him.

8

THE PEOPLE HAD GONE, but those vibes remained like an echo.

And Grayson Bryant was there with them.

"Why are you doing this, Nola?"

"I want to help Anna. Why are *you* doing this, Grayson—surely not for the same reason?"

Eric would have enjoyed the retort except that he was still trying to figure out what had happened in the past twenty minutes. After he'd dropped his bomb on the group, there was talk, most of which he missed, probably involving a date and time. The group had left, and almost immediately after that Grayson had entered.

"Nola, whatever evil plan you believe I'm hatching, know that I am concerned about Anna—and about you."

"Don't be, on behalf of either of us." Nola fussed with

the teacups and spoons, rattling them with unnecessary vigor, a rattle that harmonized with her vibes.

"Will you at least tell me what went on here?"

That was a very good question, Eric reflected wryly.

"Nothing much," Nola said with a sigh. "Introductions, of a sort. And arrangements, of another sort. They're coming back tomorrow."

"Again?"

She shrugged. "That's how this thing works. They do everything in person. No phone, no email, nothing. She doesn't even have their last names written anywhere, so I can't Google them for info. And who knows if the first names they gave are even real." Nola shook her head. "Yeah, nothing the least bit shady or suspicious about all that."

Eric let out a snort in appreciation of her sarcasm. The two stared at him and he turned red even though Nola's mouth twitched upward.

"The man calls himself Fred. He walked here," she continued. "The younger woman, Heather, rode a motorcycle; the other two had cars. The taller is Bess and the other is Pearleen. I managed to get their license plate numbers, in case we might need them." And now Nola turned to Eric. "What did you find out?"

Eric wished with every cell in his body that Grayson were not there. "One of them," he blurted. "I got . . . something . . . very strong . . . very strong . . . from one of them." He added, in a rush, "I don't know which one." And then, in almost a mutter, "I'm sorry. That's as much as I know."

Eric felt Grayson's vibes shift slightly as a signal that the man was likely about to unleash a lot harsher sarcasm directed at himself, but Nola once again intervened. "Well, OK, then. So we come back tomorrow. And you—" and to his astonished delight, Nola was speaking solely to Eric, "see if you can figure out which one of them it was."

"Which one of them was what?" Grayson interjected. "We don't know what that reaction means, Nola." Unspoken, but clearly implied, was the rest of his thought: *or if he knows what he's talking about.* He couldn't exactly blame Grayson for being skeptical. Eric didn't even know their names. And he'd already cried wolf once, with Grayson on the train. Nola's vibes were at odds with her neutral expression—suggesting that her neutrality was a mask for skepticism.

"We don't know a whole lot, this is true. So we come back tomorrow and find out some more." She pulled out a mass of keys from under the checkout counter and jangled them. "And now we go home." Again turning to Eric, ignoring Grayson, "I assume you need a ride?"

"Actually …" Grayson again. Vibes and voice slick. He turned to Eric, ignoring Nola. "I understand you do the circuit out in the Bay Area?"

Eric did not recall having told Grayson about his poker playing, though of course he seldom retained much about spoken conversations. Perhaps Grayson had been checking up on him. Regardless, Eric refused to give the man the satisfaction of having surprised him, so he merely nodded.

"There's a game I know about tonight. You won't want to miss it."

The way Grayson said it was neither as a suggestion nor as a challenge, though Eric struggled to figure out what the man's motivation was. Grayson seemed . . . curious. Like someone performing an experiment.

He continued, "I can take you there and get you home. No need to bother Nola, who clearly likes to do things on her own in her own way."

Eric knew he'd been trapped. He couldn't say no without looking like a wuss, yet once he said yes he'd look, well, like a man who'd just walked into a trap. He avoided Nola's eyes, looking squarely at Grayson as he answered. "I like doing things my own way too."

It wasn't quite the suave, tough-guy line he'd hoped for, but at least it happened to be true. Grayson nodded. "I have no doubt of that. And that's why I think this poker game will be of great interest."

It occurred to Eric later, as he sat in the silence of Grayson's car, that the man had not specifically said it would be of great interest to Eric himself. He had a feeling that was on purpose.

THERE WAS ONE TIME he'd gotten in trouble at a game. One of the players was a guy Eric couldn't stand, a guy who had

seduced a girl Eric liked enough to think he might want
to see her beyond a one-night stand. The player—and he
was that—treated the girl cruelly, not physically abusing
her but leaving her emotionally distraught to the point
of serious depression. Eric wanted to take this guy down,
badly, and the guy knew it, probably counted on it being
a distraction to Eric. But Eric wasn't distracted. He beat
the guy, soundly. He then was himself beaten—physically,
punches to his face and chest, not hard enough to do any
real damage but hard enough to scare the crap out of him.
The guy thought Eric must have been cheating; how else
could he win so consistently? Like anybody else, Eric had
seen hundreds of fights on TV and movies, but when it
happened in real life it was a horrible shock. He hated to
use the word "traumatic," but no other word could describe
the experience.

That trauma now seemed laughable compared to the
situation he found himself when he agreed to play poker
with Grayson Bryant.

Back west, Eric had played a lot of guys in baseball
caps. Some were students, while many of the others worked
in tech. The game Grayson brought Eric to that evening
seemed more like a "gentlemen's club" sort of bunch. It was
in a house in one of the more affluent neighborhoods in
Redfort, and the men were closer to Grayson's age than Eric's, many of them a lot older. As per his M.O., he registered
very little about their physical appearances or anything they

said; he simply nodded through introductions, sat in the nearest chair, and waited for the game to begin.

The game was five-card draw, not Eric's favorite and a somewhat surprising choice, but it hardly mattered as far as his strategy went. When the deal began, he quickly went around the table. A major, B major, C major, D . . . minor . . . that was Grayson, of course, who seemed to deserve a minor key. When the last card went down, Eric waited to see what changed.

Nothing too drastic, as usual in the early rounds, though F major likely had the best hand given his above-average jump in notes. Eric vaguely registered his own cards—a pair of something, that was about it—and settled into the familiar process of the game.

The game went on, the hours passed, until finally, and not surprisingly—in the back of his mind he wondered if Grayson was engineering everything that happened— it came down to Grayson and Eric. After the third-to-last player went all-in and lost, Grayson nodded, held up his hand, and said, "Eldy Rules."

There was a sudden sharp spike of interest in the vibes of the men standing around the table. "I don't suppose you know that? They might call it something different out west," Grayson continued smoothly. When Eric said nothing he went on. "Eldy means 'LD,' or 'last ditch.' It was the nickname of one of the founders of this particular upstate New York circuit. When the last two players call Eldy Rules, the stakes go beyond money."

Eric dimly perceived that a thick piece of expensive stationery and a fountain pen had been placed before him. He vividly perceived that his breathing had faltered until a faint, ragged gasp escaped him. Grayson pretended not to notice. "Write down what you wish to wager. Write down *whatever* you wish to wager. If you bet your LD and win, that's what you win. If you bet your LD and lose, the reverse happens—subject to the winner's interpretation. It can be anything. Anything."

Worlds, sinister ones, were contained in that single word.

"There have been some very interesting interpretations over the years. If you were to write, say, 'Your entire net worth,' and lose, I could decide that you owe me your own net worth—or mine." Though Grayson's face remained impassive, Eric sensed the man's smirk at the difference between those two figures.

Grayson picked up his pen, staring at Eric—daring him. Eric picked up his pen, wrote three words on the paper as though he were merely jotting down three things on a grocery list, and pushed the paper and pen aside. Amusement breezed through Grayson's vibes as he did the same. The papers were collected. Grayson dealt the cards.

Eric had fixed on Grayson's vibe patterns since the start of the game, and he felt confident. He barely glanced at his cards as they came to him, and when the last one was dealt, he waited.

Nothing happened.

Eric's eyes darted up. Grayson was looking directly at

him—and not at all at his cards, which he had left face-down on the table.

Eric knew his face must have betrayed his emotions at that moment, but it hardly mattered. Grayson had figured it out; he had figured out how to beat Eric—which was to let Eric beat himself. He had to make his own decisions based on his own hand. He knew he was defeated.

LEAVE NOLA ALONE.

That was what he had written on the piece of paper. Presumably that was what he himself would now be asked to do.

Grayson was driving Eric back to his mother's apartment. Could he possibly feel any more puny in the man's presence than in this particular situation? Not likely, he reflected.

"She's asked for my help," he protested weakly. "If I cut out now …"

"You don't have to 'cut out.' Stay in for now."

Eric waited for whatever else was coming—because he knew, of course, there would be more.

"I want you to convince Nola that I need to be there tomorrow too." He didn't wait for Eric to respond—after all, what could he say? "Let me set a few things straight. I've known her longer than you have, and more important, I understand her in ways you couldn't possibly understand. What you do is completely different from what we do. You measure and interpret. We absorb. What we experience becomes part of us. Don't even pretend you know what that's like."

Eric never thought he'd pretended such a thing. He just . . . liked Nola. Enjoyed talking to her. That was a rare thing for him. He didn't imagine some deeper connection; he wasn't even sure it was possible for him. Hell, the cynical side of him didn't think it was possible for anyone except in wishful-bordering-on-delusional thinking. That's how he thought of Grayson at this moment. Nola's vibes around Grayson did not suggest someone who was comfortably in sync.

But he'd lost the last ditch bet. Once again, the advantages he thought he possessed had only turned against him in the end.

9

"ERIC, ARE YOU ALL right? What's wrong?"

Eric closed the door behind him and stared at his mother, stared a good long time. "Mom. Can you hear vibes?"

She looked confused—but only for a moment. Slowly, quietly, she said, "Is that what you call it?"

She knew.

"No, I can't," she said after a long pause. "But your father could."

Eric registered the words without reacting, though he fleetingly wondered: did this mean everything made more sense or less? He moved like a sleepwalker into the living room and sat down. His mother followed, he knew without seeing her, and sat at the other end of the sofa. She said nothing for a while.

"You have to understand where he was coming from, Eric," she finally said. "He belonged to a generation that thought you were either sane—meaning you were like everyone else—or you were crazy. That generation didn't understand things like depression or anxiety disorders. If you were depressed, you snapped out of it, shut up about your problems and went to work. That's what he tried to do, only he had a very hard time doing it.

"Did you know your father wanted to be a trial attorney? He couldn't even get through law school, though, because the . . . vibes, you call it? They made it hard for him to concentrate, to focus. He couldn't be in a room with other people when he studied, and in classrooms he felt like he was going mad. He gave it up after just one year, went into his father's business."

Eric's grandfather had been an electrician. Honest work, Eric's father had always said, with the conviction of someone who doesn't want to consider any other possibilities. Eric shook his head and tried to smile at the irony but failed. If his father had tried harder, he could have made his vibe-reading work wonders for him in a courtroom. He could have read a jury like nobody's business. He'd always know when someone was lying on the stand. Eric imagined his father sitting on the edge of his seat, watching courtroom drama scenes on TV shows, excited at first, hopeful, then, after he'd had to give up on his dream, angry, embittered, ultimately defeated.

"So now you know," his mother added carefully, "why he treated you the way he did."

"No, Mom, that's crap. If he knew what I was going through, he should have understood. He should have tried to help, somehow. Why did he have to make me feel like a freak?"

"Because he felt like one. I'm not saying he was right. But people treat others the way they feel the world treats them."

"Well, why didn't ..." He hesitated.

"Why didn't I do something about it?"

Eric nodded.

She nodded too, as though this was the question she deserved to be asked. "I didn't understand, not at first. I didn't know what either of you were going through. You were too young to tell me and he wasn't able to. He just couldn't do it. I had to figure it out from bits and pieces of things he'd said, ways he reacted to other people, ways he dealt with you."

"He bullied me. That's how he dealt with me. Did he think that would help?"

"No. He thought—" His mother sighed. "He identified with you."

Eric stared at the flower arrangement before him as though it had started to talk.

"Yes, Eric," she continued, again answering a question she thought he should have asked. "A person doesn't have to hear 'vibes' to have empathy and understanding. When he looked at you he saw himself—his disappointments, his frustrations. It made him angry, but he wasn't angry at you. No, that doesn't excuse him. Take is as an explanation—or at least part of one. I don't think any person can be fully explained."

"Why didn't I ever hear any of this before? Why wait until after he's gone to…" He trailed off. Eric already knew that answer: he hadn't stuck around to hear any of it. He'd left before any of them had a chance to try.

"Eric …"

"Mom, look, I'm . . . sorry. I know I've been away a long time." He had no idea what to say next. It would have been nice to say something *like but that time has been put to good use*, except it would be a blatant lie.

It didn't matter. Even if he lied—and she knew he lied—she'd say the same thing she said now. "It's OK, Eric. It's OK. I understand."

10

A DARK ALLEY, WITH STRANGERS. It would have been a terrifying situation, except that the motley group assembled was not even remotely threatening. Even Grayson, the most suspicious of the bunch, made Eric feel more prickly humiliation than fear. The man had bested Eric and was there despite the fact that neither Eric nor Nola wanted him there. But Grayson had won the wager, so Eric had to persuade Nola that the man's presence was necessary.

"We could use the help in case, you know, something bad happens," Eric had said lamely when both Grayson and he appeared outside her door.

Nola stared at them, hard, then shook her head and marched off to her car. She didn't speak to either of them for a good thirty minutes. Finally, Eric sensed her anger abating, and she spoke. "I tried to do some digging on our four new friends. Pearleen is an unusual name, so I started with that, though I got the spelling wrong at first. It's actually her name, Pearleen Montgomery. She's a registered nurse at a clinic. There was a photo of her on the clinic's website, so it's definitely her. Divorced, fifty-one years old, no children. I had a hunch about Fred, thought he might be a professor, and he is, or was, rather, at the community college. His photo's still on their website as well. Fred Shetland, his full name. Quit a couple of years ago, no idea why. Somewhere in his mid-40s, based on the year he got his Ph.D., not married. No criminal records on either of them. I had a hard time with Heather, since that's almost certainly not her name, but I asked around at certain retail stores and restaurants and I think she might be a server at a bar called Wymy. Somewhere in her 30s, as near as I can guess—probably too old to carry off that look and lifestyle." She grinned for the first time that evening. "Not much else on her. Struck out completely on Bess. I tried searching for 'Elizabeth' in various venues that seemed possible but didn't find anything."

Grayson's vibes showed him just as astounded as Eric was. "You found out all that since yesterday?" Eric said.

She shrugged. "Don't be impressed. It wasn't that hard."

Not for you, Eric wanted to say, but he was wary of looking too worshipful—and inept—before Grayson. Grayson wasn't paying attention to Eric, though; he was smiling in that cat-about-to-eat-the-canary way Eric had come to detest. "This is why I called you, Nola. Well, this is *one* reason I called you."

Nola did not respond. The car was silent again, and remained that way until they reached their destination.

Eric thought about the information Nola had provided. Which of these vague and basic details might be significant? Why did Fred quit his job, and what was he doing now? How did a registered nurse end up getting involved in this weird death ceremony? Heather seemed to be part of an edgy crowd, or at least gave that impression; might she know of the thrill-kill group? Who in the world was Bess?

Good questions; no way at the moment to find answers, other than his ability to read vibes. He hoped that would be enough.

When they found the alley, they discovered the other four were there already. *Who knew freaks could be so prompt,* Eric thought and then felt ashamed of himself. The irony was not lost on him, his calling them freaks. But they had a choice in their "freakishness" while he did not. They'd chosen to participate in activities that caused them to be ostracized from mainstream society. Or maybe they hadn't chosen. Maybe each of them had a "thing" like Eric's vibe reading.

One of them might also be a murderer.

"Let's get started," Nola said. "By the way, this is another new member, Greg." She gestured at Grayson, who nodded. The group barely acknowledged him. They were ready for business. Their vibes, Eric noted with frustration, were uniformly tense, no aberrations to detect. He needed someone to stand out, and so far no one was.

"I don't know how Anna used to do this," Nola continued, "but I'm going to run this, er, session the way I do it.
I hope this is acceptable to you."

More nodding around the makeshift circle. The group
looked much the same as they did the last time he saw them,
though he was sure Nola was picking up all sorts of amazing
things about them much in the way of Sherlock Holmes.
She probably knew their nicknames, their favorite colors,
what each of them had for breakfast. Eric couldn't remember what *he*'d eaten for breakfast, if anything. Something
with the letter "b" in it, perhaps.

He tried to focus as the group, led by Nola, moved further into the dingy alley, past broken chairs and beer bottles.
Grayson was close on her heels, to Eric's annoyance, followed by Heather and Fred, then Bess, and finally himself
and Pearleen. Pearleen was far more agitated this time than
last, but then so were the others. Still, she managed to look
up at him and give him a reassuring smile. He smiled back,
feeling about the least smiley he'd ever been.

Nola jerked to a stop. Everyone knew: she'd found the
trace. The others responded immediately, moving around
her; Heather gestured to Grayson and Eric to be part of the
circle. Eric expected them to hold hands and start chanting
or something but they each merely bowed their heads, so
Eric bowed his too. He didn't need to look at them to ob-
serve them in the one way he knew how.

And then something else started to happen, something
he had not expected and could not understand.

They were disappearing.

Six people stood before him, and six sets of vibes slowly faded away.

Horrified, Eric looked up and tried to scream. Instead he found himself, too, fading away to darkness.

ERIC OPENED HIS EYES and saw his mother. No, it wasn't his mother, it was one of the women in the group—Pearleen, that was it. She didn't look all that much like Angela Lafferty, but her vibes had been the ones that seemed familiar, and now he knew why: they reminded him of his mother.

He did not know why he was lying on the pavement.

"Eric." It was Nola's voice. Her lovely face appeared. "This is probably a dumb question, but do you have any idea what just happened?"

Eric sat up. Nola and Pearleen crouched beside him; the others were a few yards away. He wondered where Grayson was but then realized he was standing with the rest of the group. Why hadn't his presence registered right away?

Eric rubbed at his eyes. To his horror he realized there were tears on his face. He had no idea what happened, and he cringed to think how dumbfounded and pathetic he must look.

"I don't know. Everything was just . . . gone, suddenly." He was having a hard time speaking. Some vague but insistent thought pushed into his head just as he gained full awareness of Grayson Bryant's vibes, and he knew—he *knew*—that whatever had happened, Grayson had caused it somehow.

He needed to communicate this to Nola. But Nola had turned away and was conferring with Pearleen.

"I don't like his color," Pearleen was saying, and he remembered that the owlish woman was a nurse. "He hit his head when he fell, too. I think he should get this checked out."

Nola was nodding. Eric wanted to reach for her face, hold still her nodding, lean closer and whisper that she was in danger, that Grayson was the cause of this danger, that he—Eric—could protect her. He couldn't protect anyone, of course; he couldn't even speak properly at the moment.

"Should we take him to the ER?" Nola was asking.

"No," Eric gasped. *I have to protect you . . . somehow.*

Pearl looked down at him sympathetically. "It's OK, sweetie. I can get you a discounted rate for the uninsured at the Willard Clinic. That way you don't have to face a big bill for an ER visit."

How had she known Eric didn't have insurance? Something wasn't right here. Something was happening. He just wished he could do something about it.

The next thing he knew, he was being lifted into a car. People were talking, vibes were happening, but Eric couldn't focus on any of it. The car door closed. Someone got in and started up the engine. And suddenly Eric registered the vibes.

He should have figured it out: the easiest thing to notice with vibes was change. One person's vibes had changed the most when Eric made his announcement about going to where Lasky died: Pearleen. She'd gone from calm to crazed in seconds. She was doing the same thing right now as she drove them away from the others.

It was quite possible that he had just found Sabrina Lasky's killer.

11

"TELL ME THEIR NAMES."

"You need to let me go."

"First tell me their names."

"I don't know what you—"

"Yes you do and you know it. You and your little whore girlfriend, you were both in that gang, so you know all of them. Tell me the names."

Eric tried to open his mouth. *Nola isn't a whore. She isn't my girlfriend. We're not in a gang and I don't know what names you're talking about.* All of that was what he meant to say but only a faint squeak came out of him. Suddenly he understood: the names of the gang members. Pearleen thought he was Max, the dead girl's boyfriend.

"I don't know anything about Sabrina Lasky, Pearleen. I never met her. I'm not her boyfriend; he's somebody else."

As soon as he said it, he knew it had been a mistake. "How do you know that? Stop lying. You're with them. Tell me what I need to know and I won't hurt you."

Eric did not believe the last part for a second. He opened his bleary eyes and took stock of the situation. He was in a room that looked to be a guest bedroom—clean, sparsely furnished with a twin bed and a dresser—although he had no recollection of how he got there. He'd been put on the bed and was not restrained. It was probably Pearleen's house, and if that was true, Pearleen most likely had neighbors who might hear if he yelled for help. Of course, they might not do anything even if they did hear. The person who might do something was Pearleen. She had a handgun pointed at Eric's chest.

He tried to play to her professional side. "Whatever I was drugged with . . . I think I'm having a reaction. I can't—"

"I didn't drug you. I don't know what happened to you back there but it was a lucky break for me."

As far as he could tell, she was telling the truth about that, but the mystery of why he'd blacked out would have to wait until he figured out how to get out of this dangerous mess. He tried a different approach. "Is Anna OK?"

It seemed like the right question. Her vibes softened to confusion and concern. "I don't know. I don't know what happened to her." Then they hardened. "Maybe your people got to her."

"They aren't my people. I'm not with that group."

"That's what your girlfriend claimed at first, even though she knew I knew. She jumped—she died—rather than tell me anything." She paused, not out of drama but uncertainty, though it certainly had an impact. "You'll die too if you don't."

Eric tried to recall anything he'd read or heard about how to deal with violence. Keep the violent person calm. Don't beg or plead, but speak to them in a gently authoritative manner. They will be very suggestible, believe it or not, so take advantage of that if you can. "You are not going to kill me," he said softly. "I will try to help you. But to help you, I need to be able to focus. I cannot remember if you are threatening me; it is too stressful." The words sounded silly even to him, but hopefully he managed to make them sound convincing.

It seemed to work at least a little. His captor leaned against the door, head in hands, as though exhausted. "I didn't hurt her. She jumped. I think maybe she joined our group because she felt guilty." Eric nodded slowly; this was probably true. Sabrina had already felt terrible for what happened, and when faced with the consequences, she fell apart. "I didn't mean for it to happen the way it did. I just need those names. I need to find them."

"I know you do."

"They killed him."

Him? Would it be prudent to ask who the "him" was? Eric didn't think so, at least not at the moment. "Killing is wrong. No one should kill another person."

"But they're getting away with it."

"No, they will not."

A glimmer of hope appeared in her face, as though Eric had made a royal proclamation that must be carried out. Then that hardness returned. "No, they will not. I'm seeing to that."

Pearleen Montgomery's vibes made it clear she meant what she said. The question was why. Eric figured he had nothing else to lose at this point. "Tell me about him."

As deceptive ploys went, it was a weak one, along the lines of the hero in a thriller getting the villain to reveal his entire dastardly plan to buy more time to figure out an escape. To his surprise, it actually worked—at least as far as the plan-revealing part went. "You and your pack of animals killed a good man. I know you probably thought of him as garbage because he lived on the street. He wasn't garbage. You're garbage. Joe Montgomery was a good man."

Montgomery. Son? Brother? Husband? Nola had said Pearleen was divorced—did she keep his name, and would she care this much about an ex-husband?

"I still loved him, even after all the hell he put me through, the drugs, the cheating, jail, even after he left me, I loved him." Yes, clearly, she did still care. "He was sick, not bad. He needed help. But instead he got treated like garbage—by filth like you! Tell me their names."

"Max," Eric blurted out of desperation. Why did it feel like a betrayal? In truth it was the only name he knew—though he knew now that Max had not killed Sabrina.

"Sabrina's boyfriend's name is Max. He's with the group that killed Joe. Pearleen, that's all I know. I don't know any of the others. Maybe Max does, I don't know that either."

He held his breath. Was there an easing of the tension in her vibes? "Can you find him?" she asked.

Eric hesitated; he hated to say "I don't know" again, but he truly did not know how to find Max.

Glass crashed somewhere in the house. Pearleen sprang to her feet and whipped around, eyes on the door. Eric knew this might be his chance to get the gun away. He didn't move. He was lying not quite close enough to her to make a flying tackle, and he doubted he'd be quick enough, in his still-woozy state, to get to her before she could turn back toward him. Besides, there could be help coming for him. Surely Nola would not have just let this woman take him away, knowing she might have been responsible for Sabrina Lasky's death. She would have followed them, or at least gone to the clinic and, not seeing them, called the police. At the very least, there would be someone else to help him subdue Pearleen.

A window was thrust open. Someone tumbled into a room, thudding on the hardwood floor. The vibes seemed familiar, but Eric couldn't place them. The voice that spoke, however, was instantly recognizable. "You killed her. I'm coming for you, bitch."

Eric did not have to find Max. He was right there in the house, approaching the door to this room.

Pearleen stepped back from the door and waited, holding the gun with both hands, body turned slightly so she could see Eric in her periphery. Her eyes were wide, her body trembling.

Eric's thoughts raced. He did not feel drugged by anything except adrenaline now. Max almost certainly had a weapon, but if it was a knife again and not a gun it would do no good. Of course, if he had a gun, that wouldn't make things any better.

The doorknob rattled. Pearleen had locked it. "I have a gun," she shouted, going into a crouch. Her voice sounded confident, but her vibes betrayed intense fear.

A shot splintered the door above the handle. Max had a gun too.

A gasp choked out of Pearleen. She looked at Eric, and despite the illogic of it, she seemed to be asking him what she should do.

Eric had to do something, but didn't know what—or to whom. Pearleen had threatened Eric's life; Max only cared about Pearleen, though he likely did not care who might get caught in the crossfire. Pearleen had already caused one death, albeit indirectly, and was looking to cause another— possibly two, counting Eric. She wanted the names of the gang members, presumably to hunt them down and kill each of them as well. Something about her plans seemed not entirely right to Eric, though. The resemblance to his mother stuck in his mind. As far as he knew, his mother would never do anything remotely close to threatening lives. And yet, a big fucking loser like Eric's father had tied her down to a miserable life. Still she stuck with him to the end, even beyond the end, still defended him and took his side. Pearleen perhaps was doing something similar with Joe.

Eric's mother never wanted to hurt anyone. She definitely would never want to kill anyone. Would Pearleen?

No. He suddenly knew that with absolute certainty, even though it was completely irrational. She wanted to, took steps to do so, probably thought she would be able to given the chance, but face-to-face like this, just about point blank, she would not shoot first.

What about Max?

Eric had never been in a situation even remotely close to Max's. He had never loved anyone so much as to want to avenge their death, to kill for them, in doing so probably risking death. Desperation: that was what Max was feeling. When had Eric ever known that?

Something clicked in his head, and he realized he did know that, though not first hand. His father. His father drank out of a desperate need to escape what he thought of as a failure of an existence. He drank because he felt he had nothing left to lose in life and so he drank himself to death.

Max was willing to kill and to die.

Even if Max didn't have any beef with Eric himself, Eric couldn't just let him kill Pearleen.

He gestured toward her, holding his hands up and away from his body as well as keeping steady eye contact, and slowly moved between her and the door. Confusion frizzed through her vibes. Eric held his hands palm out in what he hoped was a reassuring gesture. Then he turned toward the door.

When Max slammed into the door and burst it open, Eric lunged at his torso, knocking them both into the hallway. The gun did not leave Max's grasp. He fired again. Pearleen screamed. Her gun clattered away from her. Eric seized Max's gun hand and pushed it to the floor as hard as he could. "Pearleen, run!" he screamed.

He heard Pearleen fall heavily to the floor. He smelled blood.

"Get the fuck off me!" Max shouted at Eric.

Max was stronger than Eric and would overpower him in seconds. He heard Pearleen moan and realized she was still alive—but not for long once Max got away. If he could just get Max outside, away from Pearleen—without getting shot himself—well, if he could do that he might just win the Nobel Peace Prize. With that wry thought, Eric bit down on Max's wrist, the one holding the gun. In the brief moment when the bite caught Max by surprise, Eric pushed away, stomped on the gun hand for good measure, and stumbled down the hallway.

"Motherfucker, you're fucking—" another gunshot. "—dead."

Heat, like a steaming iron searing his side. Eric ignored it, slammed into the front door, yanked it open, fell out into the yard.

"Police!"

Don't shoot, Eric screamed in his head, and then he saw the figures of Nola and Grayson off in the distance. *Grayson. I have to stop Grayson.*

"Don't shoot!"

Max stood above him, pointing his gun down at Eric. Two uniformed cops stood thirty yards away, ready to fire at Max. "Don't shoot," Eric said again, and he meant it for everyone there, Pearleen, Max, the cops, even if each of them believed they had something huge to gain by shooting. But if they took a shot, someone would die, and if someone died . . . *Stop Grayson.*

Max fell to his knees, dropped the gun. No shots fired. The cops swooped in, one taking Max and the other disappearing in the house only to reappear with Pearleen.

For the second time that night Eric found himself looking up at Nola. He waited, but Grayson did not appear— nor did he or Nola disappear.

Eric exhaled for what seemed like the first time all night, and closed his eyes. He had done it. What, exactly, wasn't clear at the moment, but frenetic vibes danced around him, he knew it had been necessary.

12

"How did you know she wouldn't shoot you?"

It had been one very long night. Eric had gotten treated for his wound, given his statement, found out that Pearleen was in stable condition. Nola was there to take him home (after having called his mother to assure the poor woman that her son was OK). Grayson was nowhere to be seen. Eric hoped he would remain that way.

"Did you get it from that vibe-reading thing?" Nola continued as they pulled out of the hospital parking lot.

Eric considered her questions. He struggled to come up with an answer, not because he was tired but because he didn't know. "Not entirely. Part of it was that, but part of it was, I don't know, just trying to figure out how they thought about things, how they felt, Max and Pearleen both. I guess I tried to make it make sense to me."

"Hmm." Nola nodded thoughtfully. "Funny. What you and I do is so different, but one thing's the same for both of us: it only goes one way, what we do. We can perceive, but we can't convey, or create, or give back. At least not immediately."

Eric remembered how fervently he'd wanted Max not to shoot—how he wished he could send those vibes into the boy's head, knowing that he couldn't. "Yeah. So we have to figure out how to do that in other ways."

"Yeah." They stopped at a red light, watching other cars go past. "Which, actually, in the end, is not so different from what everyone else does. We perceive the world first, then try to figure out what to do in that world."

Eric had never quite thought of it that way, but it certainly made sense given everything that had happened. Who knew if it would continue to make sense once the shock wore off.

After a few minutes of silence, Nola spoke again. "I'm guessing Max is going to play fall guy for the thrill kills. He'll confess to having done all of them even though he obviously wasn't the only one. Anything to be part of the group. I get it," she added. "Few people on earth are immune to the need to fit in. Funny thing is, most of the time I hate having this weird thing that makes me different, but sometimes I think it's lucky."

Eric mused over her words as the car moved through the night. He knew what she meant by lucky; being so markedly different in some way meant that at some point in your life, probably earlier than most people, you recognized that you didn't have to try to fit in, since you never fully would. Was that really a lucky thing, a good thing? Maybe. At any rate, he was feeling pretty lucky to be alive right then.

"In case you're wondering, Max had been there at the alley, watching us. When he saw Pearleen take you away in her car, I guess he went on a hunch and followed you. We saw him take off after her. We tried to follow you too, but we were held back by the group."

"The group?"

Nola nodded. "Yeah, it's kind of a milder variation of Murder on the Orient Express. They're all in on it, or at least they all suspected that Pearleen had some connection to one of the thrill-kill victims and decided not to interfere. They're the last people I'd think of as approving vigilante justice, but as Bess put it, 'Sometimes how we heal isn't simple or easy.' This was after she got Grayson in a choke hold. Turns out she teaches martial arts."

"Wow," Eric muttered. Secretly he was relishing the idea of Grayson being overpowered by an older woman, though he tried not to show it—much.

"Yeah," Nola agreed with a hint of a smile as well. "To be fair, it wasn't just Bess—Fred was also restraining him. Heather meanwhile was looking at me like she decided to stop being vegan and start emulating Hannibal Lecter. The only way we got free was I told them about Max, said Max

was probably going to kill Pearleen. Finally they let us go."
She looked over at him to catch his eye. "Eric, I'm sorry
you had to go through this. You should never have been
involved, certainly not to the point where your life was at
stake."

"I got myself involved."

"Yeah, and got yourself out of trouble, too." She looked
back at the road and smiled again. "When I open my private
investigation firm, you got yourself a job."

Her vibes suggested playfulness, as did her voice, but he
wondered if there was any substance to the idea and not just
lighthearted joking.

"You didn't laugh," Nola said. "That's good. Maybe this
nutty idea isn't so far-fetched after all."

"I don't think it's far-fetched at all," he said eagerly. "You
could totally do that. You're, like, a natural at it."

"I don't know about that, but if nothing else there may
already be a case to solve. We still have no idea where Anna
is, after all."

"Yeah, about that. Grayson is hiding something," Eric
said cautiously.

"I know that."

He was taken aback. He'd been cautious for fear that
Nola might defend the man, but of course she knew Grayson better than Eric did.

She continued. "He told me next to nothing about why
Anna came to see him right before she disappeared. He said

she was upset about something and seemed not well, but he wouldn't give any other details other than to say it wasn't about Lasky. Wouldn't say how he knew that, either."

"Well, neither Pearleen nor Max seems to know anything about Anna either, so maybe Grayson is telling the truth at least as far as that goes. I still think he knows something he's not telling, though."

"Yeah," Nola said grimly, "he's got a pattern of that. Still, no one else who knows Anna has declared her missing. She has extended family all over the place, apparently, and they haven't said anything to the police."

"So maybe she just wants to be missing from certain people?"

"That's my guess."

He hesitated, not sure how to phrase what he needed to say next. "Nola, this whole . . . trace thing. There's something seriously wrong with it."

Immediately he sensed her guard up. "What exactly is wrong with being a tracist?"

"Nothing is wrong with being a tracist, but Nola—at the alley, something happened to me to make me flip out like that. And I think it has something to do with the whole trace business. I can't sense trace, but you and Grayson can, and Grayson—well, he's different from you, isn't he, in how he deals with it?"

Slowly Nola nodded. "Yes. He . . . takes it. Absorbs it, uses it like a drug."

Eric returned the nod. "Well, what if when he does this he ends up sort of, I don't know, also taking some living energy? Something blocked my ability to read vibes in that alley, made me pass out. At first I thought maybe Pearleen drugged me, but she didn't. Nola, I think it was Grayson."

Nola stared at him, but there was no hostility in the look or her vibes. "Grayson drugged you?"

"No, I mean, when he took the trace, his vibes got messed up, somehow. All of yours did. There's something just not right about all that, though I can't really tell you what or why."

Nola was silent for several minutes, then said simply, "Another mystery."

They had reached the apartment where Nola and Mrs. Lafferty lived. "Man, after all this stuff that's happened to you, now you get to go to a funeral," Nola said. "This is some week you're having."

"Actually, it's just a memorial service. The funeral was last week. I, uh, missed it on purpose." He confessed. "I wasn't ready to deal with coming back here."

"I can't imagine any of this has helped."

It had, in ways Eric couldn't explain.

They made their way through the parking lot, into the lobby, up the elevator to their floor. "Do you know what you're going to say at the memorial service?" Nola asked.

A week ago Eric would have said "nothing." He'd had nothing to say about his father most of his life because he'd always thought of his father as someone who wanted nothing to do with his own son. Now he said, "I don't know."

Nola reached out, put a hand on his shoulder. "You'll figure it out. That'll be your next mystery to solve."

She let go and went into her apartment.

Eric paused before knocking on his mother's door. Maybe he'd "figure it out," like Nola said, but it seemed far more likely that his father would remain a mystery to him forever. Still, acknowledging that seemed like a victory, of a sort. Not knowing was better than not caring. He didn't always know what to make of people's vibes, or their words, or their actions, but he knew he could at least try to find out.

He knocked on the door. "Mom. I'm back.

Sync

1

WE ONLY TOOK WHAT people wouldn't miss. That's a greater kindness than life usually offers. Kip and I certainly weren't given that kindness in our lives, but we still tried to be decent people. At least he did, and I did for a while, until things went bad.

We needed money. Doesn't everyone? Especially when you're nineteen and trying to stay in college and it's not like most of the other nineteen-year-olds who get help from their parents. I don't resent them; it's actually nice to know there are some decent parents in the world—some decent people in the world—who want to help their kids get an education. All Kip and I had was each other. That sounds lovely, like song lyrics, but song lyrics don't often say how "having each other" means getting through premed and onto med school without a little help.

Or in this case, helping ourselves.

Here's how it worked: we would knock on the door, a person would answer, Kip would hypnotize them and I'd go in and rob them. It wasn't really hypnosis, Kip insisted, not like people always think of it, like on TV or in those bogus acts they do at parties and stuff. This was the real thing, and it was more like putting someone in a gentle trance—only Kip didn't use the word "trance" either. The way he described it was he'd simply get them focused on one thing, the sound of his voice. No, not even his voice—some sort of vibration he was making in his throat while he talked to them. They didn't even realize he was talking after a while. You couldn't make them cluck like chickens or anything stupid like that because they weren't in a state of suggestibility so much as a state of calm focus. Whatever, it still sounded like hypnotism to me, but Kip called it "syncing"—synchronizing their brainwaves to the vibrations. Like I said, whatever. The main thing is, it worked without fail.

And I didn't "rob" them, not much. I only took a small amount of money and food. That was what we agreed on. Whatever cash I could find and two or three things I found in the fridge or pantry, things that wouldn't be missed much because the people had several or the stuff was pushed to the back and they'd clearly forgotten about it anyway. Yeah, sure, once in a while I was tempted by a cute pair of earrings or a scarf, but that just wasn't right—plus, OK, I freaked at the idea that I'd be wearing the thing in public and the lady of the house would happen to be there and see me and start pointing and screaming or crying because I'd stolen some treasured heirloom from her. Stupid, yeah, but at least we could sleep with fairly clear consciences.

"Good morning, ma'am. We're botany students from the university and we're doing research on lawn grasses in the area." That was his favorite, and it was a good one. For some reason the people in these houses not only loved talking about their lawns, they also loved thinking there was something special and research-worthy about them. For others it was just enough that we weren't going to try converting them to our cult or to hit them up for money—at least, not that they were aware of.

Ten minutes. That was all I had. Kip could hold the sync state for a lot longer than that—hours, he'd said, "basically as long as a person can go before they have to pee"—but we figured it would look strange if a neighbor happened to notice Kip and the person at the door standing there, staring at each other and not talking for a long time, so we agreed on ten. I would even time it, not that I had to, but as dumb as it sounds, it added to that adrenaline rush. In and out in ten minutes. The person Kip had synced would stay in a pleasant fog for a few minutes after we left, so our getaway would be clean. They wouldn't remember much, but they would feel nothing bad—as though they'd been meditating.

Later, in Kip's ancient Nissan several blocks away, he finally asked, as though it took him an effort to admit what we'd done.

"What'd you get, Emjay?"

"She must have just gone to the ATM. She had a lot of twenties in her wallet. I only took three. And look!" I showed him a box of Corn Chex, some bananas, Campbell's tomato soup. "She had tons of this stuff. Must have just gone to the store, too. Look—there's cheese! We can make grilled cheese with tomato soup!"

Kip's big brown eyes got huge when he was excited, and those eyes were like twin moons after I said that about grilled cheese and tomato soup. He looked excited, yes, but also relieved, because I only took a little bit. That's Kip. He doesn't want to hurt anyone. That's why I told him these things after we finished, assured him I'd stuck to the rules. Normally someone that nice would irritate me, but Kip always made me want to be a better person, just for him, so I could see him look at me that way.

Later on, after the sandwiches and soup, I revealed the other thing I took—a really good bottle of wine, or what looked like one, French words and a line drawing of a castle on the label. There'd been a couple of cases worth in a floor-to-ceiling wine rack. I figured by the time I revealed the wine, us happy and full and ready to tear each other's clothes off, he wouldn't mind so much that I stole it, especially when I suggested drinking it together in the bathtub. I was right—he definitely did not mind.

Of course, Kip was the one taking all the risks. The person he synced with would get a good look at his face but only a glance at mine. We'd go up to the door together—seeing a couple made people less suspicious than if just one person knocked—and Kip would do the talking. He'd launch into a story about being a student doing "sustainability research" that compared certain types of lawn grasses or some damn thing, it hardly mattered. The minute he started talking, he started syncing, and I slipped into the house. As soon as I got out and back into the car, Kip would say, "Thank you so much for your time," smile, stop the sync, wave, and walk away. The person at the door would look mildly confused but smile and wave back. How could they not? Kip looked like an angel, the boy these people hoped their sons would become and their daughters would date. I looked like the girl they warned their sons about and, given my spikey hair and arm tats, the girl they hoped their daughters wouldn't date either. We're well into the 21st century but certain things still freak out people who live in nice houses.

Kip learned to sync from his grandfather. The grandfather had these books, he called them "white magic" books, as opposed to black magic. "White magic is supposed to be about helping people, healing them," Kip explained to me once. We were lying naked on a futon in the exact center of the floor of our studio apartment, like it was an island. Our island. A tropical island. We were naked not just because we were having a lot of sex but because the A/C didn't work and it was July. "These books are sort of like medical textbooks, really, only I guess it's an alternative sort of medicine. They're very old and valuable. My grandfather treasured them so much. I couldn't believe it when he wanted to share the knowledge inside these books with me."

The gist, Kip's grandfather had said, was that the human body is amply capable of healing itself if we could just let it do that. Unfortunately, a lot of what people do to "heal" injuries and stop pain actually prevents the body from healing. Syncing allows the body to ignore all distractions and focus on repairing itself. "It isn't magic," Kip insisted. "It's science. But it seems like 'magic' to most people because most people don't understand it. Healing isn't about attacking the thing inside you. It's about getting better and carrying on."

Kip wanted to be a doctor because his grandfather was one, because his grandfather wanted to heal people. Me, I wanted to be a doctor because I aced all my science classes in high school and because I wanted to show every last asshole in my old neighborhood—including the family of assholes I grew up with—that I wasn't the worthless little shit they liked to tell me I was. Yeah, maybe not the purest reason to go to med school. My schmaltzy personal essay that got me into the State University of New York's premed program sounded more like Kip's story than my own: an inspirational elderly family member who served as a guiding light and encouraged me to pursue a career—nay, a lifetime—of healing. I think I was laughing as I wrote it, either that or puking. But nobody else needs to know the truth but me. Well, Kip knows most of it, though he chooses to believe only the good parts. That's Kip.

I guess goodness, like a lot of genetic stuff, skips a generation, because Kip's mother is a total shit. She hates me, of course, thinks I corrupted her precious boy or something. She wanted Kip to go to an Ivy League school instead of a SUNY, never mind that Kip's grades were only so-so. She likes to think Kip gave up Harvard for me so that she could have a solid reason to hate me. She has to hate someone. Kip's father left her a while back, but she can't hate him because that would be admitting he actually left her and wasn't ever coming back. Yeah, she's that delusional.

Kip's mother wasn't wealthy, though she lived like she was—except when it came time to help Kip through college. Kip grew up firmly middle class, which makes it even stranger that he turned out the way he did. He got it, you see. He didn't pity "the poor," nor did he blame them for their own problems. Poor people—like my family, like all the people I knew until I left home—still were people to Kip. So were rich people, which is why he accorded them equal respect with everyone else, even when we stole from them, even when we—or, really, I—violated the privacy of their homes. He did it because we were this close to being evicted one month and that close to starving another.

I did it for those reasons, but also because it fascinated me. This was how normal people lived. These were their homes, stocked with food and clothing, gadgets and books. Their homes were full, clean, and bright. Their homes were happy places.

Or at least that's what I thought until I entered the pretty brick house with the big picture windows. Those windows were framed by rich, burgundy-velvet curtains, and I remembered thinking, If this were my house, I'd keep those curtains open all the time, especially on a sunny day like today, so I could look out the window and see the lawn, because there weren't broken car parts on that lawn, broken bottles, old needles, or anything else old or broken or bad. I thought a house like that meant never having to see anything bad ever again.

I was about as wrong as I could be.

2

How KIP'S GRANDFATHER GOT those books of white magic is a story Kip sometimes told me when I fell into those black-hole moods of mine. I guess you'd call it "depression," except a depression is just a dent in the earth and this felt more like a crater. Besides the books, there were letters, notes, and a diary, and from these came the full story. The story wasn't exactly a happy one, at least not the way it ended, but maybe that's why I liked it and why Kip told it to me. It was honest. The truth isn't nice just because you want it to be, and when I feel lousy I don't want to hear pretty lies. They'll just make me feel worse. Kip knew that. So he'd tell me this story.

Kip's grandfather inherited the books from his own father, who came to the U.S. from Germany around the turn of the century as a young man. Frederick Schlage came through

Ellis Island to New York but quickly left the city for upstate. He was not a city boy; he preferred tall mountains to skyscrapers. He settled in a small but picturesque town called Redfort, married a local woman, and began his practice as a family physician. Unfortunately, he ended up spending as much time giving medical care to his wife as to his other patients. Kip wasn't sure what her illness was—likely some form of cancer, though she'd been described as "sickly" or "unwell" or one of those other typical euphemisms of the times. As she got worse the doctor found he needed help. He couldn't balance his wife's needs with his practice. So his wife's cousin, a nurse, came to live with them.

Eventually his wife died. She was still young, but no one was surprised. They'd seen her frail body, her face twisted from the never-ending pain. Neither was anyone surprised when six months later the doctor married his wife's cousin and nurse. This was how things went. What might have surprised them was that this young woman was not only his wife's nurse but his own pupil. In Sarah Coyle, Frederick saw more than patience and kindness; he saw intelligence, aptitude, and genuine skill. He taught Sarah to sync, at first as a way to help ease his wife's pain, and then so that she could help him with his practice. She took some of the simpler, more routine cases, especially the women and children, leaving him to focus on more difficult and complex medical matters. At night they would talk about their work together. He listened to her reports about the patients she'd seen, and she learned about the procedures and treatments he'd done. Sarah became his partner in more than one sense of the word, and it was more satisfying than he had ever thought possible.

In the few photographs that exist of Frederick and Sarah, he's a surprisingly cheerful, almost comical-looking man. He's grinning through a thick moustache and his eyebrows are raised as if in mock surprise. She's more serious, with dark hair and eyes and very pale skin. She's almost as tall as he is, and she looks like someone you would not want to fuck with. But you can also see how he might fall in love with her. She's got spunk, and there's fire in those coal-dark eyes. Anyway, that's how Kip put it. After hearing the story so many times, I guess I believed him, even if I knew he was entwining their story and ours. That wasn't a bad thing—up to a point.

How we met and became a couple is a boring story: high school, lab partners in chemistry, skipping prom to fuck all night in his backyard treehouse, of all places, his mother not fifty yards away in her house, fuming. She'd wanted Kip to ask some sweet dull girl that she could boss into wearing the prom dress she'd picked out and posing in a million asinine photos for her scrapbook. As soon as she met me, Marilyn Pearson knew that wasn't going to happen, so she basically ignored Kip the entire week of prom. That worked out well for us; Kip snuck food, beer, candles, and a sleeping bag out to the treehouse and never even had to pretend he went to the prom because bitch mom didn't care anymore. Still, we weren't too different from every other couple in high school, disappointing their parents, sneaking around to have sex, thinking they'd invented sex, thinking there was nothing else in the world but each other.

How we got into the syncing scam wasn't much more dramatic. It started with a hotdog. We both wanted one and didn't have enough cash. Nobody would believe Kip came up with the plan—everyone would prefer to think a "girl like me" would be the one to suggest stealing—but maybe Kip thought up the plan because even he thought I was going to steal the hotdog, and this scheme would at least keep me from getting caught. Kip asked the guy at the hotdog stand—Nathan's, if that helps justify the theft—for a dog. The guy took Kip's money first, probably used to kids getting their food and then taking off without paying. But when he came back with Kip's hotdog, Kip was ready to sync. Then I stepped forward to take the first hotdog. Anyone seeing us would never suspect anything was amiss. When Kip stopped the sync, the guy "came to," or whatever the term is, and saw a nice-looking boy patiently awaiting his hotdog. So he went and got another.

That was how it started. It ended at the pretty brick house with the windows.

We were having a fight that morning in the car. No, not really a fight; it's hard to fight with someone who never raises his voice and never actually says—or believes—that you're wrong. Anyway, Kip told me he'd decided to go full-time at the hospital where we worked as nurses' aides. He'd be given the big-deal title of healthcare tech. I could tell he thought it was a great thing but knew I wouldn't think it was a great thing at all. He was right. "That's great, Kip, but it's gonna be awfully hard to do that and school, don't you think?"

He nodded slowly. "Yeah . . . well, about that."

"You're dropping out," I interrupted. He nodded again. "Kip, don't be a dumbass. We don't need money that badly. We already talked about this. We can both get through without one of us having to work full time."

Now he shook his head. "That's not why I'm doing this. Look, Emjay, you belong in college. This is easy for you. You should be a doctor—you'll be a great doctor. Me, I'm already struggling. It's not exactly gonna get easier from here, right? I'd rather do this instead."

"You'd rather clean bedpans?"

"It's more than that, Em."

"Oh right, checking vital signs in the middle of the night and getting yelled at by the patients for having the gall to make sure they're still alive. Yeah, that sounds amazing." I looked away from him, ashamed of my retort. We were still parked in front of our apartment so I made a big show of fishing the keys out of my jacket pocket and fussing them into the ignition. I hated making him feel bad for this choice since I knew he'd stick with it, but I was disappointed. I wanted it to be us together through it all; this would change things.

Kip got it, of course. "This won't change anything," he said, putting his hand on my arm.

"How do you figure that?"

"I mean, yeah, it changes some little things but not the things that matter. You still get to be a doctor. I still get to help people in my own way. We'll be together. What else matters?"

What indeed? I sat for a moment in silence, wondering why this bothered me so much. Was I being as shallow as Kip's bitch mom, wishing Kip would aspire to more for himself? I didn't think so. Kip's being a good person meant more to me than his being a doctor, or anything else. Did it irk me that he'd made a decision without consulting me? Hardly. There were times I had to remind him that he did, in fact, have a mind of his own and could do stuff by himself. Maybe I worried this change would emphasis the biggest difference between us. Kip did things for other people while I did things for myself. If I said that to Kip, he'd deny it and say what a good person I am and all that, but I'd always know the truth.

As if to emphasize that truth, I said, "You won't get paid for that gig for a while. We need money now. Let's hit another place."

As soon as I said it, I knew this would be the last time. Once Kip was gainfully employed he'd want me to focus on my studies. And while that was all well and good, a part of me felt the letdown. It was exciting, this thing we did. Illegal, sure, though it would be nearly impossible to prove I was breaking and entering when, for all intents and purposes, it sure as hell looked like these people let me waltz right through the door. But Kip knew better and it bothered him. "Grampa wanted you to use your powers for good and not evil, Kip Skywalker," I used to joke when he told me the story, and Kip would laugh and do some Star Wars voices and I'd say something crude like *the force is strong in this one* while rubbing his crotch. Still, I knew he was stretching his powers of rationalization pretty far to justify what we did. Me, I didn't justify it. I just got my kicks, and like any addict, I was going back for one last hit.

WE PARKED AROUND THE corner from the brick house. As soon as the man answered the door—a man, tall and perhaps middle-aged, was all I noticed—Kip started syncing and I slipped through the door. Wealthy, this one, not ridiculously so, but you could see the guy had taste. Art on the wall that had to be originals and not just prints, furniture that looked good even more than it looked pricey, lots of books, lots of light.

Light, that is, in every room but one. At the top of the stairs, a door was open but no light shone into the hall. The room was probably an office rather than a bedroom, and offices were frequently cluttered—which meant they were good for picking over. I headed into the dark room.

Even with the shades pulled and the lights off, I saw her. I saw her and stared. I froze. And then I turned around and ran.

"Why won't you tell me what happened?"

We were in the car. We hadn't pulled away from the curb. I knew we had to get moving. Yes, we were around the corner from the guy's house, but you never know if someone might figure out that something strange had happened and come looking for us. I couldn't move, though, not after what I'd seen. I couldn't speak either.

Kip watched me anxiously. "OK, you don't have to tell me what happened, but…" He put his hands over my hand on the steering wheel. "Why don't you let me drive? I'll take us home, or maybe . . . maybe we can get some coffee, or pancakes, or something."

Pancakes. I always craved pancakes when I was agitated. After exams we'd hit IHOP and splurge, and I'd eat so much I never wanted to see another pancake again—at least until the next time I got all antsy and stressed. Kip, pancakes, so much sweetness and loveliness in my life that never lasted, never quite took me away from the past, because nothing ever could.

I pushed off his hands. "I'll drive. I'm not helpless." It was the last thing I said to him.

Because he was looking at me—because he was looking after me—he didn't see what I was doing. He always thought I was so wonderful, so strong, so whatever the hell else he thought. He didn't see that I'd ignored the stop sign and drifted into the intersection. And he didn't see the car coming toward us, fast, from his side. How could he see it when he was looking only at me?

3

Kip's grandfather could have stopped telling him the story at the point where the happy couple got married, leaving him to imagine the happily ever after, but of course he didn't. What happened next in the story was everything went to hell. Someone in town discovered that "Dr. Schlage" was not really a doctor—or so they claimed. Perhaps it was merely that his credentials weren't recognized in this country, but regardless, the authorities began to investigate. They discovered that the good doctor was also trusting a lot of his work to someone else without proper credentials—and a woman, at that.

Here's the killer irony of all time: their suspicions were based on the fact that she was too good at what she did. Her work at midwifery in particular was astounding. How was it possible the mothers did so well, experienced so much less pain, recovered so much more quickly? Of course this was because she could both treat them medically and sync them to ease the pain. Even though this was very nearly the 20th century, whispers of witchcraft began to grow.

Popular and beloved as the doctor was, he had a German name and a German accent in a time when people weren't keen on any names that were "different," any accents at all, and German ones in particular. They had him arrested and jailed. It happened fast. This was a small town without the kind of backlog seen in big cities. At first they did nothing to Sarah Coyle, figuring that she had simply been manipulated by him. They ignored her protests, her frantic warnings about the doctor needing her help for serious heart problems. They insisted that the doctor must be stopped from continuing his practice while these affairs were sorted out.

He died in jail that night.

And Sarah Coyle vowed to avenge his death.

HIT AND RUN. WE were hit, the other driver ran. I didn't know why, since we were—I was—partially to blame for being in the intersection. But the other car was almost certainly speeding, and who knows, maybe the driver wasn't insured or had a record or something. Or maybe they saw what happened to Kip and freaked out.

Kip wasn't wearing a seatbelt and the car had no air-bags—we got it for cheap because the airbags were defective. Kip's mother screamed at me about that, even though she'd had her choice of cars to drive up here to identify the body and could have given him one when he started college. It would have been as easy for her as giving away an extra, unused and unneeded napkin at a picnic.

The screaming had been at the hospital; later she showed up at the apartment. "Get out of my way," she hissed when I opened the door, even though I was standing clear of the doorway. She went through the motions of pushing past me but ended up just waving her arm at me, bracelets jangling, as though pointing me out to someone else in the room. But no one else was there; it was just me now.

"This is how he had to live because of you," she said disdainfully, even though the place was spotlessly clean, if sparse. "And then he died because of you." She whirled around, waiting for me to respond so she could cut me off and spew more venom at me.

I didn't respond. There was nothing she could say that I hadn't already thought myself, that I wasn't still thinking. I could have told her she might as well look in the mirror and blame herself, but what would be the point? You can't make someone else face a hard truth if you can't face it yourself.

She waited a beat, then made a disgusted noise and stomped off, trailing Chanel No. 5. Seriously? Kip's mom in a nutshell: someone who had the presence of mind to douse herself with expensive perfume before going to see her dead son.

She didn't say another word the whole time she was there. I heard her yank open the hallway closet, pulling our things out—our things, Kip's and mine, only now they were no one's things because there was no "our" anymore. She just couldn't wait to grab everything of his, including a few things that were mine. Thank god the lease was in my name or she'd have kicked me the hell out then and there. I probably would have let her, too, so I wouldn't have to be alone there.

Luckily the books were in an old backpack, so she probably thought they were textbooks. She's so stupid she wouldn't know something valuable if it fell on her. The books were obviously old and precious; she should have seen that even without opening them. Instead the stupid bitch went right for the electronics—Kip's laptop, his stereo, his gaming equipment, his TV—cheap old junk he'd gotten for free from friends. She only took the clothes after she got all the other stuff. Who the fuck does that? Me, it's my kid, I'd pick up every damn sock of his, clean or dirty, and hold on to them all the way back home.

Instead, I held on to those books.

4

THE NEXT YEAR WAS very, very long. It should have been a time of letting go, I suppose, but it was just the opposite. I spent the year reading those books, learning what Kip had learned about syncing. It was my way of holding on.

Most of what the books talked about was incomprehensible to me, so I skipped to the part about syncing—which, luckily, was one of the earliest of the translated chapters and also one of the shortest. I fleetingly wondered what else the books might teach me, but I put that question out of my mind. I put a lot of things out of my mind that year, but maybe not the things I should have.

Some of the sync chapter sounded kind of new-agey, surprising given how old the books were, but I guess "new age" is a misnomer, as Kip once pointed out. "All those hippie-types didn't discover anything new but just re-claimed stuff that was ancient and gave it a groovy contemporary twist." I can still see his face, the way he pursed his lips and raised his eyebrows comically at the word "groovy." "Grooooooooovy!" I repeated, pushing my face into his.

To sync, the book said, you had to learn to focus, to center yourself, to get mind and body synchronized. Yeah, whatever. Other parts of the chapter were far more grounded. I had to learn circular breathing, for example, something good jazz sax players learned so they could keep a steady $O2$-in-$CO2$-out stream even while producing an equally steady stream of crazy notes. I bought a penny whistle at a dollar store and practiced with that, probably driving the neighbors nuts with endless renditions of "London Bridge is Falling Down."

And I practiced—a lot. I stopped caring about the stuff we were studying in school and instead used campus as my personal laboratory for my own self-made curriculum. In large lecture halls I practiced on the people sitting next to me, attempting to draw them into the sync and then asking for a pen or a piece of paper. If they responded, the sync hadn't worked. If they simply looked at me without responding—and they appeared calm and relaxed rather than startled by my question—I knew I was successful.

Only once did I scam someone with the sync, though there were plenty of chances, and only because money was getting tight. I went to the bank—to a teller, for the first time possibly ever, instead of the ATM—and withdrew everything in my account, all of a hundred and five dollars. The teller counted out the money from the cash drawer and the instant she turned to me to count the bills again—all official-like, the way they do in case customers think they're incapable of counting—I started the sync. Instantly her face changed: relaxed but not slack, calm yet focused. It was fascinating, to tell you the truth. I could see getting creepily addicted to syncing, even more than hitting houses for cash and food. I held the sync only briefly, just long enough to scoop up the bills and shove them into my pocket, and then I released her.

This was risky, as it always had been since the first hot dog heist. Sync didn't mean the person was open to suggestion or forgot everything that happened before or during. At best there might be temporary forgetfulness, like when a person is interrupted in the middle of doing something requiring concentration, and that was what I counted on. As is typical after a sync, the teller looked mildly confused but not distressed, like someone who woke up from a nap and wasn't quite sure what time it had gotten to be. I stood there looking cheerfully at her with my wallet open, clearly no money in the wallet. "If I could get three twenties and the rest in fives, that'd be great—thanks!"

The teller cheerfully complied and I got the hell out of there as quickly as I could without attracting attention. I felt bad for her—no doubt she'd get in serious trouble later on when her cash drawer came up $105 short—but I needed the money. I knew I could never set foot in that bank again since they probably had it on video that I took money I wasn't entitled to. Never mind that the bank charged me pretty much every time I tried to do something with the money I was entitled to.

What was it like to sync someone? Impossible to describe, not because it's such an intense experience but because it's so subtle, like whispering sounds that could be words but aren't quite. You sort of . . . sing, deeply, through your lungs and throat, but you don't make a sound, and you do something like sliding scales until something clicks, until you know you've hit that right "note" that matches your brain waves, or something like that, near as I could figure out. I didn't think about it too much; I simply tried to get it right.

After one semester of practice, I mastered the sync. That's when I dropped out of school. I didn't need school anymore; I'd learned what I needed. I also took the full-time position Kip was going to take. It was easy to get; they were hiring by the dozens, it seemed, and I had just as much cred as Kip. I worked hard, learning everything I could there as well. Took vitals, gave sponge baths, moved patients on and off bedpans. Later there would be phlebotomy and a few other specialized skills that required training, though this was laughably easy compared to the self-imposed training of syncing. And the job provided me ample opportunity to sync in a way that was real and beneficial. Every time I interacted with a patient, I synced. And every time I finished and waved goodbye, they had a smile for me, a real one, not the kind of smile that masks pain and fear and exhaustion.

Even though my work was stellar, my supervisor couldn't quite figure me out. The patients always said they felt better after talking with me, even though we never said much to each other and some of them weren't even sure of my name. I certainly didn't know all their names, or anything personal about them; beyond syncing I kept my emotional distance from them—from everyone. Once my boss gave me a hard look and said, "Frankly you always seem so—sullen." I gave her an equally hard look and told her that maybe that's what patients liked about me. If you're in pain, who wants to see someone who's bouncy and chipper? You want to tell them go fuck themselves. She didn't answer me, just shook her head and walked away. And in truth I don't really believe that myself. If you're in pain, you don't care how people around you look. You just want the pain to stop. That's why they liked me: through syncing, I helped them stop the pain.

I didn't intend to stay at the hospital, though. Nobody liked me but the patients, and everyone else was starting to watch me very closely. I knew it was only a matter of time before something bad happened. It always does.

Sometimes, though, the bad thing happens because you want it to happen.

❖

THE JOB WAS LISTED as "medical assistant." It covered a lot of duties, not all of which I could do, but I applied anyway. It was a long shot, but the only shot I had. And then, in one of the few lucky breaks I've ever had in my life, I got the job, without even an interview, in part because hardly anyone else applied. The job was with a new non-profit foundation whose mission was to provide healthcare services to migrant farm workers. The head of the foundation had inherited a wad of money, and right now he was pretty much the entire foundation. Its mission was mildly controversial; some people bristled at the idea of offering free medical care, especially given that some of the workers were probably illegals. What's more, the main services provided weren't exactly glamorous—or even all that interesting, from a healthcare professional's standpoint at least. These were farm workers, and they suffered a lot of work injuries: broken bones, strains and sprains, burns, cuts, and bruises. A sprained ankle to most people would be a minor annoyance; you'd be given painkillers and crutches or a boot and told to stay off the leg for a few weeks. These people would get none of that; staying off a leg for a few weeks meant no pay for those weeks, and that wasn't going to happen. But stay on the sprain doing hard manual labor, and it might get worse—to the point where it might never get better. Without medical treatment and advice, they could end up crippled for life.

All of that comes pretty much verbatim from the foundation's mission statement. Funny thing, it kind of reminded me of stuff Kip used to say, the more disillusioned he got about becoming a doctor, shaking his head over MD candidates who went in for the money and prestige and glory and ended up being "shills for Big Pharma." Kip would have loved this job so much. I didn't plan on loving it—I didn't imagine I could love anything ever again—but I planned on doing it very, very well. This was exactly what I wanted. I could use syncing to help people who really needed it, and there wouldn't be anyone around watching me suspiciously, no one around at all except the patients—and the doctor.

The head of the foundation was also its only doctor. I knew his name, of course, but I always thought of him as the doctor—like in that that show, Doctor Who. God, Kip loved that show; he'd always get a man-crush on whatever new actor was playing The Doctor. This doctor wasn't anything like Doctor Who—too serious, no whimsy at all, and despite his work, no real yearning for adventure—but that wasn't a problem for me.

There's something you need to know about the doctor, though, something important—and something you need to know about me.

It was the doctor's house that Kip and I hit that one last time.

When I looked into the darkened room at the top of the stairs, I saw a woman. She was sitting at a desk, back to me, and crying, the muted crying of someone so weary it almost takes more energy than they have left to show their sorrow at all. Her hand covered her face, her soft breaths were ragged, and her shoulders were trembling slightly. I looked at her shoulders and then at her neck. I saw clearly, even in the dim room, the huge and vivid bruises encircling that neck. My eyes fell to the desk in front of her, where a crumpled necktie lay. She clutched one end of it in the hand not covering her face. I knew someone had just tried to choke or strangle her, and it was almost certainly the man downstairs who was being synced by Kip.

And then suddenly she looked up and saw me in the mirror. Instead of being scared, instead of pleading for help, she hissed at me, enraged. *Get out of here. Get OUT. OUT, BITCH!*

I got out. You know what happened after that.

What you need to know about me is this: My father was a wife beater. They all were, the fathers back where I grew up, no big shock there. For a while my brothers and sisters and I lived in fear that he would come after us, but he never did. I'm not sure why he reserved his abuse solely for our mother, but that's how it was. Us he treated with gruff indifference, when he dealt with us at all. Her he loved, passionately, and beat with just as much ardor.

Just as bad as his brutality, though, was the fact that she seemed almost . . . proud of it, sometimes. Like she was suffering for love, like all of that showed how much she cared about him. Sometimes when we looked at her—her bruises and scars, her fractured bones—she seemed almost scornful of us, defiant of our pity. But who knows, maybe she just felt she had to adopt some sort of attitude that wasn't cowed and defeated so we wouldn't start hating her even more than we hated him.

I wanted no part of that, thank you very much. I escaped as soon as I could. Still it's impossible to truly get away from something you lived with every day of your life. I wondered how fucked up it had make me, living every day with two people who did or endured terrible things and called it love.

My father was a respected man, even if he wasn't a doctor. He still got away with the things he did. So did the doctor—if the doctor had done anything. I wasn't sure. But I was damn well going to find out.

THERE'S A PART OF the story Kip never told me, but it's there in the books, one of which was a personal diary written by Sarah Coyle. I doubt Kip's grandfather told him this part of the story. Perhaps he figured Kip would read it on his own.

After her husband died in jail, Sarah Coyle wanted revenge. She didn't care that she wasn't prosecuted, that the authorities had gone easy on her. The men who put her husband away considered her an innocent victim, or else they didn't care much what happened to her because now she had no husband and no money and no way of making a living, and that was considered punishment enough. But none of that mattered to her; all she cared about was getting back at the men who, in her eyes, killed the man she loved.

It was easy. All she had to do was get alone with each of them, one at a time, and sync them into submission. She had a list: the man who leveled the charges, the witnesses who spoke against Schlage, the judge who ordered Schlage jailed. One at a time, she found them. She asked them to meet with her privately—crying, begging forgiveness, begging for help, acting every part the helpless female. When she got them alone, she took action.

When they recovered from their synced state, they would find the note.

I want you to understand just what you did. You need to know just how much he helped those people—and how much good you destroyed.

They would also find some part of them gone. A finger. A toe. Part of an earlobe. In one case, a rib, astonishingly fine work with small, feminine stitches left behind. Sarah Coyle, it turned out, had learned surgery along with syncing.

At some point I began to imagine enacting that kind of revenge on the person who killed Kip. It excited me, a more twisted version of the excitement I used to get before we hit a house. Going in and feeling that rush, wondering what I'd take.

I wanted to get back at the person who killed Kip. But I didn't know who killed Kip—nobody did, it seemed. The police claimed there were no witnesses, no one who saw the car. Obviously, I hadn't seen it either.

I went back to that neighborhood, knocked on all the doors in the vicinity, desperate to find out if anyone had seen anything, begging whoever answered the door to ask everyone who lived there, anyone who might have been there, begging and pleading until most of them, even the nicest, shut the door firmly in my face. I got next to nothing. One woman thought she might have seen an old car, a yellow one—or was it blue? (How could you be uncertain between yellow and blue?) She remembered seeing it around the time of the crash, speeding down the street, and she was sure it did not belong there. The way she said that, from the doorway of her expensive house in her expensive neighborhood, seemed pointedly meant to remind me that I too did not belong there. It might have been my car she described, after all, though my car had been black and I hadn't driven by this part of the street. These people did not need to help me; they didn't need to do anything for me. It might have been one of them who killed Kip. To them he was no more than a bump in the road, easily run over, and they'd languidly suggest that someone else must have done it, someone who didn't belong.

Just for the sake of being thorough, I asked, "Where was the car driving from, and in what direction was it going?"

The woman closed her eyes for a long time and opened them, which might have indicated deep thought but looked instead like she was wishing me gone. When she peeked and saw me still there, she frowned a little and said, "It was driving that way, and it came from there." She waved her hand vaguely in one direction and then in another.

"From where?"

The frown deepened (go away, you horrid little urchin). She pointed again: "There."

She was pointing at that house. The one we'd hit.

Only the most desperate lawyer in the world would have put this woman on the stand; nothing she said sounded convincing or believable. I didn't care. It was what I needed to hear, so I believed it.

I'd gone to every house within four blocks of that inter-section—except that one. I couldn't even look at it at first, but finally, six months after Kip's last day alive, I went back. Not to get closure, though. I wasn't entirely conscious of why I was there, but I knew I needed to be. I parked my car across the street—a car even shittier than the one trashed in the hit-and-run, if you can believe that—and I waited. I waited for several hours in sub-freezing temperatures, not caring how cold I got. It was a Tuesday; he'd be at work, and who knew when he was coming home, given most people's lengthy workdays. Finally I saw the garage door open auto-matically and a car—silver, probably worth ten times the piece of shit I was in—pulled in. I dimly saw movement in the garage as someone tall—it had to be him—got out of the car. He was alone. There were no other cars in the garage, yellow, blue, or otherwise. The garage door closed. I waited. I watched lights go on in the house. I continued to wait, not for anything to happen—nothing was likely to happen for the rest of the evening—but because I knew what I wanted to do and I knew there would be no going back afterwards.

I didn't know who killed Kip, so I decided to go after someone connected to that day, someone who seemed only tangentially connected to Kip's death but was still guilty of something. The man in that house had done something very bad to that woman. Kip had gotten killed by a car that had possibly come from that house. Maybe there was no real connection between these facts, but they were facts, things I *knew*, and had to hold on to that. And part of me wondered: what if it really was him? What if the man in the house had been the one driving the car? What if he wanted to kill us for what we had seen—for what we might tell, as witnesses to attempted murder? Or what if the woman had been driving the car, crazed with fear because the man had tried to kill her? That seemed unlikely to me, but regardless, Kip's death would still be that man's fault, in a way. I know how nuts all this sounds, but the more I thought about it, the more it started to make sense—or perhaps the more I needed it to make sense.

I found out very easily who the man in that house was: I nicked his mail. Just junk mail, though I realize it's still a felony. Once I had his name, it was simple to do some online searching for details. My plan had been to find out where he went for medical care—everyone goes to the doctor, or at least everyone who lives in a nice neighborhood like that one—and then try to get work there. When I discovered he was a doctor, I thought it would be even easier. Unfortunately, he had a private practice—sports medicine, to be exact—which made it more difficult to enact the plan. I'd hoped he worked at the hospital so I could keep tabs on him.

Then the job at the foundation came up. It was too perfect.

I don't know what I would have done if the doctor had recognized me. I couldn't think that far ahead; I had to see him first. As it turned out, I didn't have to do anything. I showed up for the first day at the clinic and the minute I came through the door the doctor barely glanced at me before he put me to work. "Emery James? Good. I need vitals on a patient right away." With that I was left to scamper after him toward the examination room.

Even after things calmed down, he showed no signs that I was at all familiar to him. That figured; after all, I had hardly recalled what he looked like either. Male, Caucasian, mid-30s. Tall, physically fit, handsome I guess. But mostly, I don't know, quiet-looking. That's about it. I did, however, remember the woman in that house in great detail. I looked for a photo of her on the doctor's desk but didn't see one.

Of course, the doctor might not have wanted something that personal in a workplace like this; he didn't seem to have much that was decorative here, much less personal. It didn't really matter one way or another, though. I know what I saw. I couldn't forget it. And I knew—I knew—the doctor had something to do with Kip's death. Now I just needed to figure out what to do about it.

5

Kip's grandfather was raised by Sarah Coyle's sister and brother-in-law. She left the baby—Fredrick's and hers—with her family and told them to raise him as their own, because she could no longer do so. They knew Sarah, knew better than to ask why, so they agreed. They also agreed that when the boy was much older, he would be given these books, for him and no one else, to answer any questions he might have about his mother and father. And then she disappeared.

The last page in her diary described the last person Sarah Coyle got her revenge on: the man who started everything, Frederick Schlage's accuser. His wife had been a patient. She'd given birth to a healthy boy with jet black hair and a happy smile—and very dark skin. The newborn was not the man's child, obviously, and to hide the inevitable scandal he lashed out at the doctor and the doctor's assistant. Sarah Coyle could not believe it. This man's humiliation was inconsequential compared to the loss of such a wonderful man as her Frederick, yet he didn't care. He went after Schlage and expressed no remorse at the man's death.

For him, Sarah Coyle had planned something special.

She seduced him. As she expected, he was too vain and lustful to turn her down. She said she needed money, desperately, and would do whatever he wanted if he would just help her out. He never suspected a thing—not even after, coming out of sync, confused, he realized he'd been tied to the bed and Sarah Coyle stood above him holding a scalpel.

She didn't sync. She cut. He shook, ground his jaw shut, then finally screamed. *Do you want it to stop?* she'd whisper. Sometimes he'd shake his head violently "no," other times nod it just as violently "yes," and still other times she could tell the pain was so unbearable he couldn't respond. She always gave him relief, always initiated the syncing. She would finish her work, then bring him out, just as she did the others. Unlike the others, she didn't leave, but kept going back at him again and again.

And each time when he came out of the syncing, another part of him would be missing.

THE DOCTOR SUSPECTED NOTHING. He didn't seem to care about my "sullenness" or anything else about me other than my willingness to work—and my syncing. He found out about the syncing just a week after I started, and it changed things before I'd even had a chance to figure out the next step in my plan.

The clinic was a small bungalow in the outskirts of New St. Genevieve—which, since you probably haven't heard of it, is a town slightly west of the middle of nowhere—but we didn't do much "business," so to speak. We didn't have a lot in the way of technology or equipment, and most importantly we had no prescription drugs, nothing you couldn't get over-the-counter. (A big sign in English and Spanish stated this on the door lest someone try to steal our "stash.") Most of the time the doctor was on the road, stopping in various locations where he knew the farm workers would be. How he knew this I didn't know, but most of the time, he warned me that I would be in charge of the clinic all by myself. On my first day, though, he was there when the boy was brought in. The boy was maybe twelve years old, and his right radius bone was bent in an angle that should never be seen in a human forearm.

I didn't think; I just acted. There's a kid in front of you in so much pain he can't even scream. What are you going to do? When his father or uncle or whoever set him down and I saw the boy had bitten his lip so hard it was gushing blood— for a moment I almost thought that was his injury, except it was hard to miss that arm—I leaned forward and synced.

He stopped pumping his legs and thrashing his other arm. He relaxed his bite from his lip. His eyes went dreamy and wet, and he almost seemed to be smiling. I glanced up at the doctor, but he was busy setting the arm. I looked over at the man who had accompanied him, but he was silent and poker-faced. I kept syncing.

The doctor set the arm and had the boy out the door within an hour. There were no beds in the clinic. The patients tended not to want to stay, some of them perhaps suspicious that they might be reported and then deported. While the doctor always urged them to get to a real hospital or at least return for follow-up visits, almost no one did. After the two left, I began to clean up, perhaps more briskly than I needed to—it wasn't like he was an HMO doctor with a packed waiting room, after all—but I was on edge, and not because of the broken arm. I'd seen far worse than that at the hospital. I was nervous about whether the doctor had noticed anything.

"Want to tell me what that was all about?"

He'd noticed. I turned around slowly. He was leaning against the examination table, arms folded. His face had its usual serious expression, but with a bit of curiosity in his stone-grey eyes.

I didn't want to tell him anything, in part because it sounded crazy but also because—well, this was the part of Kip I held closest, and I wasn't ready to share it. I stared at him, about to stall with the requisite "what do you mean?" but I didn't. I said nothing for a while.

He waited.

Finally I spoke. "It's . . . like a yoga meditation thing, only you help other people do it instead of doing it for yourself. You get someone to calm down and focus in a way that helps them heal rather than dwell on the pain." That all was pretty much true, except the yoga part.

He looked half bemused, half amused. "You're not exactly someone I'd picture being into meditation."

He was astute, the doctor. I wasn't the yoga type. There was too much preciousness associated with it, or maybe I was just lazy and needed a convenient excuse. I shrugged. "You never do know about people."

"Oh, I think you can know a few things," he said, the amusement now taking over. "There are only two kinds of people who would work at this kind of clinic. The first kind imagines they can save other people and the second kind imagines they can save themselves." He gave me a moment to think about that and then, with a small smile, he added, "I'm the second kind."

That surprised me. I replied with a lame-sounding, "Really?"

He nodded and moved around to the front of the clinic where the waiting room was—yes, we had a waiting room, even if nobody ever waited more than a minute or two for help, and then only if I was on the phone, which I hardly ever was—and gestured at me to sit down. I hesitated, then sat. He sat across from me but turned his chair at a slight angle, not quite facing me directly. "Really. And I think you are too. And I prefer it that way. The first kind is delusional and gives up too quickly. They're more interested in visions than actions."

"And the second kind isn't delusional?"

He nodded, as though I were a student who, instead of giving a rote-memorized answer, asked a challenging question of her teacher. "Oh yes, the second kind is delusional too, but in a productive way." He laughed shortly at that. "The first kind wants glory. The second kind wants . . . atonement."

The conversation was moving in a direction that put me on edge—even while it drew me in. This was exactly the subject I'd been dwelling on for the past year. "You think atonement is possible?"

"Atonement is a privilege. A person is fortunate if they can find a way to make up for their misdeeds."

"Man, I don't know about that. Sounds like, I don't know, religious dogma. Sounds like a way of forcing people to confess stuff and feel good about it instead of feeling like they're being punished."

"Atonement isn't just confession. It's action." He set down the file folder he'd been holding and stared out the window. "I think atonement is doing the opposite of what you did before. If you steal, you atone by giving. If you hurt people, you atone by taking away hurt." He seemed liked he wanted to say more, but he didn't. He also seemed to be waiting for me to ask something. We both knew what it was. I knew that asking it meant he would expect me to answer the same question. But I still had to ask.

"So what is it you need to atone for?"

He nodded again, looking at me and then away from me, though not in an evasive way, more simply out of . . . weariness, maybe. "I cared too much, in the wrong ways, and it made me do the wrong things. Here, I care the right way, as a professional doing his job, and it allows me to do things the right way." We sat in silence for a minute or two, then the doctor got up. "If it helps the patients, I'm for it. Carry on." He was talking about the syncing. I'd nearly forgotten it was what prompted this weird discussion. With that he nodded absently and left the room.

I sat thinking about what he'd said, wondering why I hadn't been able to react. Part of me wished I could have laughed in his face. Oh, that's what you did wrong, you cared too much? It sounded like the shit people tell you to say at job interviews if you're asked about your weaknesses. I'm an overachiever! I can't say no to work! I care too much! It was worse than that, though: it sounded like the shit my mother used to say. *He does this because he loves me too much.* And the way she said it, with that proud, almost haughty smile, looking us straight in the eye, suggesting that he clearly did not love us the same way. I wanted to smack her myself whenever I saw that smile, but instead I said nothing—what was the point? She was so fucking clueless.

But my mother never had an introspective moment in her life. The doctor, on the other hand, seemed like someone who gave careful thought to things—not in a useless, navel-gazing way, but simply because he was a thoughtful person. Because of this, the things he'd just said make a certain amount of sense—to the point where it almost seemed acceptable.

What's more, he found what I did, the syncing, acceptable. In doing so, he accepted me. I'd never felt accepted by anyone except Kip. But Kip was a good person, whereas the doctor was—what? He did good deeds. If I'd been the person I was pretending to be, that's all I'd know: the doctor helped people who had no one else to help them. And what did I really know? At his house I'd seen an image of something I thought I understood. Maybe I didn't understand it at all.

A cold whisper told me *You do know. He tried to kill that woman and then he tried to kill you. He did kill Kip. What is there to understand?*

6

AFTER THAT WE TALKED a little more about things,
never again quite as serious as that first conversation, but it seemed to set the tone for our . . . relationship, I guess you could call it. I don't mean we were
lovers or anything, hell no. We talked. We worked a lot and
we talked a little, mostly about medical stuff. Like Kip, he
seemed to think I needed to go to med school and become a
doctor. In between all that, he'd go back to his home and I'd
go back to mine—yet another crappy apartment, even emp-
tier than the last one—and I wouldn't do much of anything
until the next day of work.

In my apartment at night, I would think of the things
I should be doing to find out the truth—asking the doctor whether he was married or divorced or had a girlfriend,
and then casually bringing up (making up) something about
a car accident I'd seen on the way to the clinic, another

thoughtless hit-and-run, to see how he reacted. Chances are I'd get nothing; the doctor seemed like he'd been through too much, had too tough a hide, to let a casual comment jar him into remembering things he'd rather forget. Still I'd be determined to at least try. Then the next morning would come and we'd get started with work and all that would go right out of my head.

I was supposed to be planning something, figuring something out, some way to—what? To get proof that the doctor killed Kip and punish him for it? Or, if I couldn't get proof, to punish him at least for what he did to that woman? I wasn't sure any more. I was sure of the work, though, so that's what I did. It was important work, and we both believed in it, so that's what we did. Maybe it kept both of us from dwelling on things we didn't want to dwell on. Regardless, we worked a lot. We talked a little. Time passed.

And then quite suddenly I was reminded of why I'd taken this job in the first place.

I'd been there for three months. The doctor was on the road; as usual I was alone in the clinic. A woman walked in, clearly not a farm worker. She was pretty, not just from clear skin and a nice figure, but from some sort of, I don't know, assurance. She seemed to know who she was and what she was doing. I hate women like that. I admit it's a hatred that comes from envy. She strode into the clinic like she owned the joint even though nobody could have looked more out-of-place. She handed me a card. All it said was "Lantri & Associates," with a phone number and email address.

"Emery James?"

I said nothing. I never responded to "Emery," a name I detested, and I only responded to the even more despised and incorrect "Emily" to say "fuck no."

"Nola Lantri. I'm a private investigator."

It was hard not to laugh. This woman didn't exactly look like a private investigator, even if you didn't buy the TV and movie stereotypes. Pretty and assured, yeah, but she also looked so—I don't know, ordinary. Plus come on, how often does someone actually hear a line like that in real life? It can only sound fake.

The "PI" seemed to expect my reaction. She drew herself up a bit more and her tone became steely. "I'd like to ask you some questions." Without waiting for a response, she pulled a 5x8 photo from her file folder. "Do you recognize this woman?"

I looked at the photo. I made sure not to change the expression on my face. "I don't know her."

"I didn't ask if you knew her. I asked if you recognized her."

I should have lied outright, but she did catch me fair and square. I shrugged. "She looks familiar."

The PI kept silent. She was playing that game where they say nothing and hope you spill out every damn thing you know. Yeah, that was so not going to work on me. She gave a short nod, like she expected this reaction from me, and pulled out another photo. "How about this man?"

I gasped. It was impossible not to react. It was a picture of Kip.

"What the fuck do you want, lady?"

She nodded again. "Kevin Irwin Pearson." God, he hated his own name too—for a good reason. It's a stupid name. "Died last June in a car accident."

"What. Do. You. Want."

She pointed to the first photo. "This woman, Anna Villagomez, has been missing since the day Pearson died. Her car was recovered a week ago. It has been positively identified as the car that hit your car last June."

There was no point in even trying to keep a poker face. I think my jaw dropped. "She killed Kip?"

"I don't know that. Neither do the police. All they know is what I just told you: her car hit your car, and she has been missing."

"Why are you telling me this?"

She nodded again. A cool, and extremely annoying, customer. She pulled out a third photo. "Do you recognize this man?"

This was the photo I'd been expecting her to show me all along—why else would anyone come all the fuck the way out here? "Yeah, I know him. He's the doctor I work with. You know that already or you wouldn't be here."

"What is his name?"

"Grayson Bryant. Doctor Grayson Bryant. Now will you fucking tell me what the fuck this is all about?"

Nola Lantri, PI, kept her cool. "Doctor Grayson Bryant was Anna Villagomez's lover and one of the last people to see her alive. He is a suspect regarding her disappearance."

I didn't know how to react to that, either outwardly toward her or inside the privacy of my own screamingly confused brain. Was this woman suggesting that the doctor killed Anna—and that Anna killed Kip? What was I supposed to do with that?

"What does that mean, a suspect?"

"There's no secret meaning. He's suspected of having something to do with her disappearance. If you want it spelled out plainly, he might have helped her to disappear or caused her to disappear against her will."

She probably wasn't working with the police if she was willing to spell things out that plainly, so I pushed further. "What do you think happened?"

"I don't know. That's why I'm asking you these questions."

"If you're a PI, you must be working for someone—someone not the cops."

"The police are running their own investigation." A certain wryness in her tone suggested that she didn't believe the police were doing a particularly good job of it. "I'm doing this investigation in part on behalf of a private client but also in part because I have an interest in the people involved."

I knew she'd never tell me who the client was—if there

even was one—and the second part of what she said piqued my curiosity a lot more. "What interest? You know them?"

For the first time, Nola Lantri, PI, seemed uncomfortable. "It's sort of a . . . personal interest. Grayson Bryant and Anna Villagomez are . . . acquaintances. Actually, we have something in common. Have you ever heard of tracism?"

I frowned. "What, that death energy thing?"

"Yes. Grayson, Anna, and I are all tracists. We all can detect 'death energy,' as you call it, though most people would say 'life energy.'" She shrugged a very "whatever" shrug, and for a moment I unwillingly found myself liking her. "Anna and I used this ability to aid police investigations. Grayson Bryant used it for other reasons. Not good reasons."

This was interesting, but I kept my face neutral. I needed some information. "What does this have to do with anything?"

"Let's say for the sake of simplicity that he gets off on dead people."

"A necrophiliac, you mean."

She gave me a wintery smile, the kind of smile you give someone who uses a big word in an attempt to look like they're smarter than you. "Not quite. He doesn't necessarily get sexual gratification from dead people, but something comparable."

I remembered the pained look on the doctor's face when he'd returned from a bad accident. He was shaking a bit, like he had mild DTs. A man had been crushed by a tractor, his organs severely damaged, and had died just as the doctor arrived. I hadn't thought much of it, only surprise that he could still be so sensitive to death after so much time in a tough environment. Maybe that look had meant something else. "So what, you think he killed this Anna person to get some kind of sick high?"

"I don't know. I've presented all the facts I can give you. If you know anything at all regarding these two people, I would appreciate your help."

"And I would appreciate not being manipulated. Why the fuck are you trying to get me to do your dirty work for you by playing on the whole Kip thing? Why not just ask the doctor yourself?"

Again the wry look. "I won't get a straight answer from him. We have a certain history. He doesn't trust me and he knows I don't trust him."

"Well, I don't rat people out."

"Who said anything about 'ratting out'? We don't even know if he's involved."

"But you suspect him."

Silence.

"I can't help you," I said finally.

Nola Lantri, PI, surprised me once again by not playing the waiting game but simply getting up immediately to leave. She wasn't quite done, though. At the door she turned and held up the picture of Anna again. "You said she looks familiar. Do you know where you might have seen her?"

I knew exactly where I'd seen her. I didn't tell Nola Lantri, though.

7

T WAS ANNA VILLAGOMEZ who had caused me to run out of Grayson Bryant's house, Anna Villagomez whom I was thinking of when our car was hit and Kip was killed.

Anna Villagomez was missing now. And Grayson Bryant was trying to atone for something he'd done.

But one thing he had not done was kill Kip. She did that. I remember now what I'd blocked out before: he'd been watching us all the way down the street. I'd seen him in the doorway as I stomped on the gas pedal. I doubted there was any way he could have jumped in Anna's car, driven it around a different block and hit us. It was her.

This changed everything. The whole reason I'd come here, taken this job, gotten to know the doctor, no longer made sense. What made sense, what was true, I didn't know for sure—nor did I know what to do next, except wait for the doctor to return.

I don't know why I'd only fleetingly considered that Kip's killer might have been the woman in the house. I guess I always saw her as a victim, him the aggressor, and could not be shaken from that. Or maybe I chose to believe it was the person I had found, not the one still missing, since that made revenge so much easier. Except that I hadn't taken revenge. Maybe at some level I'd always known.

Revenge always seems simple at first and then ends up complicated. I wanted to get revenge on Kip's killer. The doctor appeared to be abusive, he could have been the one who killed Kip, so I focused on him. And then I got to know him better—or spent some time with him, in any case—and found out that he was as confusing and confused as anyone else on this planet. Now I was being told something that both didn't fit and yet fit completely.

And I knew I had a decision to make.

WHEN THE DOCTOR GOT back later that day, I simply laid down my cards—some of them, at least. "You don't remember me, do you."

He set down his medical bag and gave me a quizzical look. "I can only assume you mean from a time before you started working here. Should I remember you?"

I shook my head. "Probably not. It was brief, when we met. You probably remember Kip, though."

I saw a flicker of something in his face, though it quickly disappeared. "Kip," he echoed.

"He came to your house—we came to your house—last year. He synced you and I went in. We used to rob people that way. I went in, and I saw her."

The doctor might have been a marble statue, he stood so still. When he spoke, it was so quiet I almost missed it. "What is it you think you saw?"

"I saw Anna Villagomez. She was crying—and she'd been battered."

That wasn't quite right, but I still wasn't prepared for his response—or the iciness in his voice. "No, she had not been battered. You have no idea at all what you saw."

He spun around and went into his office. I stood in the waiting room feeling like I'd just been tasered or something. What the hell just happened? Before I figured out what to do next, he returned. He gestured toward a chair in the waiting room but didn't wait for me to sit before he sat down himself. I scrambled over to the seat across from him, wondering how I'd managed to let control of the moment get away from me.

"Anna is what's known as a tracist. That means …"

Ha, now I had the advantage. "I know what that means. She absorbs trace. I know you are one too."

This didn't make him wary or on edge, just—surprised, mildly. "Yes, I am. Since you seem to know so much, maybe you know that the absorption of trace is addictive—and dangerous. Anna came to me, desperate for help; she told me it was making her ill, both physically and mentally. She wanted to find a way to stop taking in trace. Eventually she came up with this idea that if she herself came very close to death and sensed the impending release of her own trace—and the impending absorption of it by her own self—she might stop it forever."

"Does that . . . work?"

"It's insane. It's beyond insane. She had absolutely no basis for this idea, much less any proof. But she was desperate. She was becoming suicidal, and no drugs or doctors could do anything about it. So I agreed to help her."

I didn't know whether I believed him or not. Abusers can come up with some pretty elaborate stories, especially the sociopathic ones. "So, what then, you tried to strangle her?"

"She asked me to." No defensiveness in his voice, simply a statement of fact, laced with sadness. "Not surprisingly, it didn't work. And that, I suppose, is when you found her."

"That is when I found her. And after that—that's when she killed Kip."

I held my breath. I was taking a risk here, but all of this was a huge risk, and there certainly wasn't any going back now.

The doctor slowly nodded as though finally understanding something he'd wondered about. "Ah ha. I see."

I bolted up from my chair. "You *see*? I don't think you *do* see. She hit our car. Kip died. Now she's missing. What the fuck did you do with her?" I was losing my cool entirely but I didn't care.

"Emery." He was the only person who had ever called me that and not gotten a look of disdain—or worse. "Why do you think I'm here? Yes, it's to do good deeds and help poor people, but why *this*? It was Anna's idea. When I inherited my brother's estate, I wanted to use it for charity. As corny as it sounds, that's what he would have wanted, though I was never close enough to my brother to figure out what kind of charity he would have wanted. Anna gave me the idea. She's Mexican-American, and she told me about the people she knows who work on the farms and go without healthcare. I started this because of her—and I'm continuing it in order to find her. I've been asking around, making inquiries, hoping to find some clues. Don't you get it? After she hit your car, she disappeared. *I don't know where she is.*"

I didn't want to hear that. "I don't believe you. You know what, doc? You once said atonement is doing the opposite of what you did before? Well, what I did before was I froze. I didn't do what needed to be done and Kip died because of it. So now I'm going to atone for that."

He was looking away from me and didn't move or speak until nearly a minute had passed. "So you plan on avenging Kip's death, do you? That's very interesting. I wish I could help you, but I can't. As I said, I'm already atoning for my own mistakes—the ones I made with Anna."

"You think doing all this good deed stuff is payment for what you did? Sorry, doctor. You don't do good deeds to atone for bad ones. You do good deeds because they need to be done."

And sometimes, I thought, *bad deeds need to be done.*

"Agreed," he said calmly, and for a startled second I thought he must have read my thoughts. "There's a famous line from *Julius Caesar*, 'the evil that men do lives after then, the good is oft interred with their bones.' We remember the bad things, you see. We forget the good. Yet the good happened, regardless of whether anyone remembers it or not, and that's why you do good, because of the effect, not because you want to be remembered for it."

Jesus, how the hell had we gotten to the point of quoting Shakespeare? And yet, the doctor's words were once again making me pay attention and think. "But you believe in atonement."

Again he let a significant amount of time pass, but I was willing to wait. I'd waited this long already. "Let me put it this way, Emery. If what you say is true, then the reverse must be true. If good deeds don't atone for bad ones, bad deeds don't erase good ones. I'm glad for that, because it means the people we've helped here have been helped in a very real way, despite any 'bad deeds' on your part or mine."

"Are you talking about bad things we did in the past—or are you saying we can keep on doing bad shit because we're also doing good?"

"You tell me. You're the one about to unfreeze yourself to avenge Kip's death."

My head was in a whirl. Too much had happened for me to make sense of it all, but I pushed everything else away, everything that had been said, everything I discovered, and focused on one thing: Sarah Coyle. I thought about Sarah Coyle, and everything was clear.

The doctor was watching me, and suddenly he stood up. "I am sorry. I have to do this. I have to stop you from making the same mistake I did. I have to keep you from using this . . . ability of yours, in a way that would end up harming you. I failed with Anna. I won't fail with you."

His words, the suddenness of his movement, caught me off guard, but I never found out what he was going to do next. At that moment Nola Lantri came through the door.

"Grayson," she said. "What did you do with Anna?"

8

'D SUSPECTED THE "HISTORY" between Nola and the doctor was complicated and involved. Now I was sure of it.
The doctor's focus swerved sharply away from me and
entirely on her. As for Nola, her eyes looked like they might
emit laser beams.

And I was in the middle of it all.

"So you think I killed her just to get her trace. Is that
right, Nola?"

"It wouldn't be the first time you thought about doing
something terrible to get trace. Isn't *that* right, Grayson?"

Neither of them moved from where they were standing,
but it still felt like they were circling each other somehow. "I
have thought about it. Addicts always think about it. That
doesn't mean we ..."

"Save it, Grayson. Don't take the stand that you never
acted on your thoughts so that makes you innocent. Your

inaction is just as bad. You've stood by while people close to you either died or were in danger of dying, and you did nothing but wait. You waited for your chance. You're worse than a predator; you're a scavenger."

I stared at her. That was a hell of an accusation to make against someone. I don't know if I agreed with Nola that a scavenger is worse than a predator, but I could see what she meant. The true villains of the world are few and can be stopped, except that most of us can't be bothered to stop them, and yeah, people who do nothing to stop suffering to benefit themselves are in some ways more despicable than people who cause suffering to get what they want. But did any of this really apply to the doctor?

I looked over at him to see what, if anything, he might be preparing to do. There was no tension in his face or body, no sign that any of this was causing him strain or stress. He was riveted on Nola, but he seemed more intrigued than agitated.

"Nola," he said, and his voice almost sounded . . . seductive. "I don't know where Anna is. She left my home in her car over a year ago and I haven't seen her since. I've been looking for her too. I know you don't believe me; it's always been more fun for you to cast me as the bad guy in everything. That's fine. Believe what you want. I'm hoping, however, that we can somehow work together on this. We both want the same thing, after all."

Nola laughed, such cold laughter it felt like the A/C had just kicked on full blast. "That has never, ever been true—especially when it comes to the most important things."

"Like trace?" The doctor's voice held a sly smile even if his face remained still.

"Yes. Trace."

The silence that followed this, and the odd way they looked at each other made me finally throw up my hands in disgust. "OK, look, people. I don't know what games you're playing with each other, but you're pissing me off with this shit."

I hated the whiny anxiety in my voice; I hoped I sounded bolder than I felt. At least I got their attention; they both turned to me and seemed to ease off from whatever weird battle they were engaged in. Nola spoke first. "Ms. James, I realize you also have a stake in this, so it's important for you to realize that if you protect Dr. Bryant, you are essentially preventing the truth from being uncovered. And that includes the truth about Kip."

Grayson made a noise in his throat—a chuckle. I cut him off. "I'm not 'protecting' anyone. I'm not taking sides with either of you clowns in whatever it is you're fighting over. Kip's dead. Nobody can change that, not you or the doc . . . Doctor Bryant, or this Anna person. Or me. So you all need to stay out of my way so I can do my work and get on with my life."

Such a bold speech. I wished I believed any of it. In any case, I stomped out of the clinic, trying to look defiant but probably fooling no one.

I was the one who felt like the fool.

Outside, I began to run down the gravel-and-dirt road. It was that kind of running you do when you just want to move fast and hard until you drop. I wanted not to think about any of this stuff, but I had to think about it. What else had I been thinking about since Kip died? When I got to the corner I turned up the county road and kept going. It was hot and there wasn't any shade. I didn't care. Finally, after a good hour of running, I stopped at the first big tree I found and collapsed under its shade. I lay there looking up into its branches, wishing so hard that Kip was with me right then. But he wasn't. Anna Villagomez killed him.

We were all searching for Anna, or at least we seemed to be. If the doctor killed her, of course he would only pretend to search. But I didn't think he was pretending. I think he really wanted to find this woman, just as Nola did.

As it turned out, neither of them found her. I did—or, rather, Anna found me.

9

Two men came to the clinic, one around my age and one older, maybe a father or uncle. I'd seen the older man before but not the younger one. "We need your help," the young man said. His English had only a very faint accent, and his words sounded more like an unspoken command than a request for assistance.

It was morning, two days after the brouhaha with the doctor and the PI. I was alone; the doctor had left a note that he would be out. That was pretty much all it said, too: out. I hadn't seen him since the brouhaha. Yesterday had been my day off, a day I spent staring up at the ceiling until noon then running through farmland for three hours and returning to collapse on the floor and resume staring.

I told the two men the doctor was out. I told them what I could do for them, which wasn't much. There was protocol I was required to follow on these occasions, but these men didn't look like they cared about protocol. They weren't going away. The doctor had explained what my options were if a potentially dangerous situation should arise in the clinic when I was alone, and I'd paid perfunctory attention to what he'd said. In truth I wasn't that worried. Syncing could get me out of those situations, or so I believed. Anyway, I'd stopped caring about my own safety the minute I walked out of the hospital alive and Kip wasn't with me.

The young man shook his head and repeated, "We need your help. We need you to come with us. There's a woman who is very sick."

"I'm not—"

"I know, you're not a doctor, you're not a nurse. I know. But this woman, she's suffering." At that moment the older man leaned over and whispered something in Spanish. The young man whispered back in that language. My high school Spanish was long forgotten, but whatever they were saying, I wasn't going with them.

That's what I thought, anyway, until the young man turned back to me. "She asked for you."

My mouth had suddenly gone dry. I choked out, "Who is she?"

"Her name is Anna. She asked to see you."

THERE WAS NO WAY I was going to turn them down after that, even though it was beyond stupid to get in a car with two men you didn't know.

They wouldn't speak to me after they gave Anna's name, wouldn't tell me anything else. They drove me there in a shitty-looking Chevy, and even though their urgency was palpable, they were clearly taking a roundabout route, probably so I'd be disoriented and not know where I was. That didn't matter. If this was the Anna I was expecting, I would only have to be there once.

We drove along back roads to the outskirts of some town, probably the same one where I lived. Their subterfuge was a little ridiculous—where else could they be taking me when there wasn't much else around? The older man, who was driving, dropped the young man and me off in an alleyway behind a row of houses. We'd come to a small ranch house in a decent-looking neighborhood. Not rich, of course, not even middle-class, but still, no car parts on the lawns, no boarded up windows, no broken bottles and needles. I heard salsa music coming from one of the other houses and a faint Spanish conversation from another. I barely registered the details, though. I focused on what was in front of me: the back door, a sparse but clean kitchen area, the hallway, and finally a bedroom. There was a bed in the far corner, and a woman on the bed.

I approached the bed. Anna Villagomez, Kip's murderer, lay there. Even lying motionless she had a certain energy, as though she had just been thrashing violently and might suddenly begin again. She was—how can I describe it?—ugly and beautiful at the same time. Those bruises were of course long gone. Her skin was smooth and caramel-brown and greasy with sweat; her hair, long, dark, matted in clumps; her eyes, dead dark but shining almost unnaturally bright. I couldn't look away from her even if I wanted to.

I stood right over her, so she'd have no choice but to meet my eyes. Yet she looked at me without any sign of . . . anything. No recognition and no emotion I could read. I opened my mouth to speak but seemed to forget everything I'd wanted to say.

Instead, Anna spoke. "It's not her."

My first reaction was to shout YES IT IS HER. This was the woman I'd seen in Grayson Bryant's house, the woman who, according to Nola Lantri, almost certainly was driving the car that killed Kip. This was Anna Villagomez, who was pointing emphatically at me and repeating, "It's not her. She's not the one."

The young man next to me held up his hand in a sort of pleading gesture. "You said she would be with him. We thought …"

"This is not the one I want." With that she turned her face away from us, and it was as though she'd dropped a heavy curtain around herself.

A sort of stunned silence filled the room. Then the young man turned to me with a pleading look on his face. "Please, miss. You need to help."

I tried to steady myself. "What's wrong with her," I asked tonelessly, even though I knew. It was all that business with the trace, just like the doctor had said.

"We don't know. That's why we brought you here."

I turned my gaze sharply toward him, but there wasn't really any nastiness in his voice or expression, just a hint of sarcasm. I took a deep breath and tried to exorcise any sarcasm from my reply. "Look, once more, for the cheap seats in the back: I'm not a doctor. I'm not even a nurse. I'm just a medical assistant. I can take a look at her but I can't do much."

"You helped my family before. My cousin, he broke his arm. He said a lady at the clinic made him feel better. Not the doctor; you. Anna, she's my mother's cousin, she has more than a broken arm. She's ..." he was silent, struggling, for a moment. "There's something broken in her. We don't know what. Please, you have to try."

I had a hard time believing what was happening. I'd been brought to the person I'd wanted to find for over a year—brought right to her. She was helpless and I was being asked to help her. I nodded. "OK. I'll try." I gave him no clue at all what I might be willing to try.

I took a step forward. "Anna." The name felt raspy in my throat and mouth. "My name is Emjay. I'm . . . here to help you."

Anna whipped around. "They weren't supposed to bring you here, Emjay. They were supposed to bring her. Nola."

The name startled me. "What do you want with her?"

"It's what he wants with her—that's what matters. She's the threat." Anna gave me a once-over. "You are not."

I wanted very badly to show her just what kind of a threat I could be. Not a threat? I neither knew nor cared what these people, Anna and Nola and the doctor, were trying to do to each other. I knew why I was there, and Anna Villagomez had no idea what I could do to her.

I also knew that if I wanted to do anything right then I had to focus and not go nuts with rage. I thought about Sarah Coyle. And Kip.

I felt a hand rest gently on my shoulder. Kip used to do that all the time; not put his arms around me, not take my hand, but instead touch my shoulder like he was leaning on me, relying on me, and yet guiding me. I needed his guidance. I turned, almost expecting to see him, but of course it wasn't him. It was Fernando—I think that was his name, the other man called him that anyway—who was nothing like Kip. And yet the way this guy was looking at me—hoping I'd do the right thing, looking for the good in me—seemed shockingly familiar.

He made a sharp gesture with his head toward the door and the illusion faded. I followed him out of the bedroom, leaving Kip's killer behind—for the moment.

"Sorry. She says a lot of things she shouldn't."

"What exactly is she saying? What's all that about 'him' and 'her'—this Nola person?"

To my surprise he answered my questions. "He is the man you work with, the doctor. Anna and that doctor used to be together. It went bad, and he started getting interested in this other lady, Nola." He shrugged. "Anna's jealous. Doesn't want to see him anymore but doesn't want her to see him either. While she's been here she's asked all of us—family, friends—to keep track of him. For a while we knew he was looking for her, asking around while he worked. Anna told us not to say anything. Then we starting hearing that this Nola lady was asking around, just in the last month, about Anna—and about the doctor."

"So you told Anna about it."

"Yeah. And when she heard that Nola was looking for that doctor, Anna got crazy." He shook his head. "Crazier. Demanded to see her. We knew that was a bad idea so we brought you here instead."

Fernando was leaving a few things out. He either didn't know more or didn't want to tell me more. I thought about whether to ask the next question, an obvious one. If I didn't ask, he might wonder why not; if I did, the answer might make things difficult for me later.

I took a chance. "Why is she *here*? Why not take her to another doctor or a hospital or something?"

He didn't flinch and his voice was steady. "We can't take her anywhere; people have been looking for her."

"People."

A hint of a sneer curled his lip, but he still looked more wry than menacing. "Yeah. There's always someone we know being looked for by people."

I assumed he meant the illegals. I didn't care, didn't want to get involved in all that, and told him as much. "Look, I'm not gonna ask about—anything else." I drew in a long breath. "I'll do what I can. In return I don't want to be inter-rupted or bothered. You let me do what I do. OK?"

He nodded, relieved. I was relieved too until he added, "You won't be bothered. But . . . you shouldn't be alone with her. She can be . . . dangerous."

I almost laughed. *So can I.*

10

K IP NEVER ONCE SYNCED me. I never asked him to. I was curious about what it would be like, of course, and I trusted Kip more than anyone else on the planet, but I still didn't want to see what it was like on the other end of things. I'm not sure why. Maybe at first it was because I saw the people he synced with as our victims and it would make things difficult if I identified too closely with them. Perhaps a tiny bit of it was respect for the way Kip saw syncing. Bad enough we were using it to harm people— even if minutely, without their ever knowing—worse to turn it into something akin to experimenting with drugs, some- thing to try just for a novel experience. That all made sense before I started syncing. But now that I could sync people, I wanted to know what I was actually doing to them. It would have been so easy to find out, but I never did.

I couldn't help but compare this to Anna, and Nola, and the doctor. They would never know what it was like to feel their life energy leave their body; they only knew what it was like to absorb it. But they could never find out, while I'd at least had that chance once. Now it seemed unlikely that I would ever find out either.

Still, syncing was very . . . intimate. Even if I didn't know what it was like to be on the receiving end of a sync, I could easily imagine it. And now that meant imagining what it was like to be Anna Villagomez. Instead of getting a Sarah Coyle-like revenge, I found myself about to attempt to ease the pain of Kip's killer. Was it simply an automatic response to someone suffering? Was I somehow hoping to rehabilitate her so she'd fully understand what she'd done—and *then* I could make her pay? I don't know. I went back in that room regardless.

The beauty of syncing someone who is lying in a hospital bed—or has just answered the door—is there's very little to distract them. Without distractions, the sync can take hold much more quickly. Anna was lying in a nearly empty room, but she looked like someone in the middle of a Wall Street trading pit. I wondered if she would be "un-sync-able," wishing I could take more enjoyment in the pun, wishing I could stop feeling so bitter about helping her to ease her pain when no one had been there to help ease mine. But that was feeling sorry for myself, and if I'd said something like that to Kip, I would have felt ashamed even if he hadn't responded in a way meant to shame me. I know, I know, there are always people worse off than you, but that doesn't help you or make you feel better. What could help me—what I hoped would help me with Anna—was taking action. And taking action means something you know is right, even if you don't benefit from it, at least not right away.

So when the sync finally took hold and Anna stopped thrashing, I felt a certain degree of satisfaction. I was helping someone. What happened later I would deal with later.

Syncing with Anna felt like swimming through gelatin. After ten minutes I was exhausted and had to let go. That was ironic, the same amount of time it took us to hit a place. After ten minutes Anna seemed to fall back in the bed even though she was already lying down, and I fell back myself, would have fallen right to the floor if Fernando hadn't been there to catch me. I was grateful but annoyed; I hadn't realized he'd been there. If he was going to be there every time I synced Anna, how would I carry out my plans?

"Maybe you should stop and come tomorrow." Fernando guided me out of the room. "I don't want you to get sick too." I heard the smile in his voice even before I looked at his face. It was a nice face, I had to admit, the kind of face that probably made him very popular with the ladies.

I smiled too, almost automatically, but also to keep him at ease. "How can I come back when I don't know where to go?"

He put his hand on my shoulder again (how I liked feeling it there; how I wished he wouldn't do it) and led me outside the front door. There he pointed to the mailbox, where the address of the house was plain to see. "We can take you back to the clinic now. Can you stop by after you finish work?"

Work. Grayson. And Nola probably watching him. And both of them perhaps watching me.

I said yes.

I WENT BACK, THOUGH it wasn't quite after work. I left Grayson a message saying I didn't feel good and was going home. Given what had happened, I figured he wouldn't call back and question me. I futzed around the apartment the rest of the day—pacing floors, looking at nothing on TV and online—and then, at an after-work-appropriate time, headed back.

I'd found Anna before either Grayson or Nola did, though of course it was completely not my own doing. It would be a challenge, betraying nothing, keeping them from knowing. I couldn't keep taking sick days forever. I wasn't sure what I was going to do with this crazy new development in my plan—which meant, I hoped, I could keep returning to see Anna. It would be easier to fool Grayson, I suspected; he would probably understand my being distant, furtive and wary. Nola Lantri was another matter. Her job was to find out stuff, and she might find out about me in the process of finding Anna.

I hated to admit it, but another reason I went back to see Anna was Fernando Cruz. I'd been so isolated for so long. My job was often solitary, and not being in school cut me off from a lot of people my own age. I had no friends, didn't hang out at bars or cafes in my spare time, kept to myself. Fernando and I might have nothing in common but our number of years on the planet, but he smiled when he saw me. It was hard to resist.

This is not to say that we swooned into each other's arms. He was guarded and so was I, for different reasons. Fernando knew nothing about me except that I worked with the doctor and had the ability to make people feel better somehow. He must have known that Anna was wanted in connection with a vehicular homicide, or at least that she was hiding from the law and not just from the doctor. But he could not have known my connection with her, because it seemed that Anna herself didn't remember. Of course I could never tell him about the hit-and-run, which meant that no matter how pleasant—how genuinely enjoyable—our interaction might be, it could only ever be superficial—and tense.

Fernando let me in and led me to the Anna's room. A female relative was there cleaning Anna up—sponge bathing, I guessed, even though Anna looked mobile and probably could have showered herself—so I waited in the kitchen with Fernando. I was annoyed that once again there were people in the house, but I hid my annoyance behind a sarcastic comment. "Nice digs. America *is* the land of op-portunity, I guess, even for non-Americans."

A stupid thing to say. I wanted to take it back immedi-ately, but of course I couldn't, so I squared my shoulders and looked him in the eye. I expected to see anger, maybe even violent anger, but he simply said, his voice cool and level, "I was born here and my parents are legal. I got a job too. Teacher's aide at Grant Elementary. Not welfare."

"Oh." Boy did that sound lame. "Boy am I lame," I said.

He smiled, which is more than I probably would have done if I'd just been insulted. "S'okay. I get that a lot."

"Doesn't make it right. Probably makes it worse."

"It isn't an insult to be mistaken for illegal, just—a mistake."

"Well, I don't know about *that*," I blurted.

Once again he smiled. "Even though you work at that clinic? You still think about illegals that way?"

"Well, they *are* illegal," I said cautiously. "Meaning they're breaking the law. There's no country on the planet just lets people in to do whatever they want. Nobody can afford to be that generous."

"Sure, but some things are higher than the law—like making sure someone who's sick or in pain gets taken care of. I'm not saying people can get whatever treatment and whatever drugs and whatever else they want, just that they don't get nothing at all, just because they're here illegally. A guy breaks his leg stealing your wallet, you don't let him lie there with his bone all sticking out. You treat it. Then you deal with the other stuff."

I made placating gestures with my hands. "Yeah, OK, sure, I'm not gonna argue with that. That's like our motto, practically: Healthcare people aren't supposed to judge, just heal. I *get* it, Fernando."

"Not everyone does."

"No, and a lot of the people who don't get it came from places like where I used to live. My old neighborhood? Full of people talking about evil brown people sneaking over the border to steal their jobs. As though picking fruit all day is some kind of treasure you'd steal, like a pirate."

"ARR!" Fernando suddenly growled. I jumped. He chuckled at me. "Aye, matey. We evil brown people be pirates! Hand over the doubloons and walk the plank!"

I actually giggled. I can't remember the last time that happened—not since Kip was alive, and even with Kip it happened rarely. I kind of hate myself when I giggle; it sounds like a fake laugh, like girls who are so hyper aware of how cute they are, they even have to laugh cute. But it felt good to laugh at something silly for a change.

That silliness, with all its light-hearted pleasure, ended as soon as I heard Anna's voice saying my name. "Emjay."

I felt chilled, hearing her say my name. She must have heard Fernando calling me that. Still, there was something in the way she said it . . . I looked at Fernando, who nodded and led me back to the room.

The woman who'd been bathing Anna was drying her hands on a towel; much to my shock, when she finished she put her hand on my arm and whispered "Gracias." I felt something like deep shame. She wouldn't be thanking me if she knew what I wanted to do.

Anna looked up at me, but then frowned when she saw Fernando. "Go away, Fernando. You too, Connie. Leave us alone." Another shock: she sounded so much like an older female relative bossing around a kid, it felt almost like a normal family moment. And yet it was nothing like that.

The woman named Connie left immediately; Fernando hesitated, glanced at me (what could I say or do?) and backed out of the room, closing the door. I figured he'd probably wait right outside, but I heard two sets of footsteps retreat down the hall.

I approached Anna's bed. She looked up at me without fear—without blinking. I said what came into my head: "You remember me."

She answered without hesitation. "You saw me." After a pause, she said again, "You saw me."

But was that really an answer? "Yes, I saw you." I tried to keep my voice calm. "What happened after that?"

At first there was silence. I waited to hear what happened after that, as though I hadn't lived through it myself.

Finally, she spoke again. "You saw me, you saw what I was. You *knew* what I was: a monster." Her eyes became unfocused, as though she were gazing inward instead of at me.

"I knew you could see my diseased mind, my sick body. You could see right into my soul and you knew that I was full of darkness, full of the souls of others, souls I had devoured, souls rotting inside my body instead of being free. You saw me. You saw me."

A spark of fury flamed in me. I didn't want to hear this nonsense rambling. I wanted her to tell me what happened next. "And so you did something about it," I prompted, my voice as even as I could make it.

Anna did not avoid my eyes. "Yes. I had to do something about it."

"And so you tried to kill me."

Anna looked impassively at me, not one readable emotion on her face. "You saw me. Because of that I understood, in a way I never did before, what I was. I needed to stop this. I need to stop this. This cannot continue."

"You tried to kill me. You killed my friend. He died because of you." I said it one more time. "You. Killed. Him."

Anna rolled her head back away, not avoiding my eyes but simply, it seemed, out of exhaustion. "And so it continued. It continues. Now he is killing me."

I had the weird sensation of knowing that I should be enraged but not feeling the emotion. This woman had killed Kip for no reason at all. She was crazy. She hadn't even been trying to kill him; it was supposed to be me. She remembered me, or at least I wanted to think she did, and she seemed about to remember what she'd done that day, but instead she spoke in empty riddles. I knew I should be shaking her, slapping her, screaming at her. *You killed Kip goddamn it so don't lie there pretending you're the victim in all this.* I should have been getting ready to make her pay, like Sarah Coyle made those people pay. It's hard, though, when they're already so far gone down the road of suffering.

While I stood there staring at her stupidly, she spoke again. "Grayson. He's killing me."

Grayson?

I thought the "he" was Kip. Now she seemed to be off on a completely different tangent. Maybe she didn't remember the hit-and-run at all. "How did Grayson try to kill you?" I asked.

"He could have killed me. I *wanted* him to kill me, to end it for me. Then he would get my trace—and he would know what I was going through. He got me on this. He needed to get me out of it. But he stopped. He didn't do it. He was stronger than I was. He was able to walk away." She started to writhe and thrash on the bed, so I leaned in quickly and started the sync.

So Grayson had been the one to get her addicted to trace, but he was able to walk away cold turkey and she wasn't. At least that's what it sounded like, and it fit with some of the stuff Nola Lantri had told me. Of course, this meant that Nola Lantri was wrong about the doctor. Obviously, he didn't kill Anna—had no idea where she was, in fact—and perhaps he'd truly given up his thing with trace.

Maybe all his talk about atonement was true and not just a lot of words he believed so he could feel good about himself. Maybe I could trust him.

Of course, I thought as I stared down at Anna Villagomez, as the sync took hold, as her face slowly unclenched itself from its tight fist of pain and her body relaxed, the doctor didn't trust me. He thought of me as the person who was searching for her boyfriend's killer. I wasn't that person any more, but I still didn't know who had replaced her.

11

THIS UNKNOWN ME HAD to face the doctor the next day. I went to the clinic, checked the mail, the fax machine, the email, the phone messages. I got out some files with information I needed to input in our database. The back door opened and closed, and the doctor entered the room.

"Emery."

I stopped what I was doing and looked at him. I owed him that much, even though I was tempted to ignore him and pretend to be working with unbelievable fervor at the data entry. I waited for him to speak since he clearly had something in mind to say.

"You're valuable to this clinic. I don't want anything to ruin the work you've done here—or the work I hope you'll continue to do. It's important work, at least in my view, and I think it's a view you share."

I nodded, though I didn't need to; he knew I wanted to keep working there.

"I think we're both people who are able to keep our personal lives separate from our work lives—under normal conditions. That said, I daresay there isn't a whole lot 'normal' about any aspect of our lives right now."

I doubted there was anything normal about our lives ever. It occurred to me that although I'd spent my life thinking of myself as different, the doctor was in a whole other league of different—as were Anna and Nola. The current situation might actually have been harder for him than it was for me.

"I want to find Anna to make sure she's OK." the doctor said. "That's all. Why do *you* want to find her?"

I answered without hesitation. "I don't know." It was the most truthful answer I could give. "I thought I knew once. Now?" I shook my head. "That's all I can tell you."

It occurred to me that I should have acted more suspicious of him; after all, he didn't know that I believed in his innocence—or at least his innocence when it came to Anna's "disappearance." I knew he hadn't killed Anna and he'd "harmed" her only because she asked for his help. But I knew that because of something I couldn't reveal. Still, I didn't want to lie or pretend any more than I had to. And how could the doctor ever guess that Anna, or at least some of her family, had been looking for me? I certainly hadn't expected it. Then again, not a whole lot of what had happened lately could ever have been expected.

I didn't know what would happen next with the doctor either. All he said was, "OK." And then, "I really wish we had coffee here."

That was a small joke we shared. The doctor refused to buy a coffee maker for the clinic, not because he objected to giving free coffee to patients but because he felt that making coffee would be beneath my position. I have to say, given some of the doctors, male and female, I met at the hospital, this was pretty astute of him; a lot of those assholes were constantly asking anyone they considered subservient to them—which was everyone—to bring them coffee. To this doctor I'd said I didn't mind, but still he'd insisted: no coffee maker. "We'll make do with overpriced Starbucks from the drive-thru."

I'd smiled then against my will. Now I simply smiled. Maybe there wouldn't have to be strained politeness between us.

The phone rang. I answered with the standard clinic greeting and heard a familiar voice. "It's Fernando. I need to talk to you."

Grayson had gone into in the back office, but he could still likely hear me. I wasn't sure if I needed to let Fernando know I wasn't free to talk, but I figured it wouldn't hurt. "Our hours are 8 a.m. to 6 p.m. Wednesdays through Sundays. The doctor is usually in weekday mornings." As in, it was a weekday morning; he was here.

"OK, I get it. Look, don't come to the house after work. I need to meet you somewhere else. Do you know the Houghton Diner?"

"Yes, that is correct."

"Can you get there at 6:30?"

"That's probably a very good idea, sir."

"OK. I'll see you there."

I hung up and busied myself on the computer. Grayson never left his office. I glanced at the clock. I had a long time to go until I found out what in the world that was all about.

HE WAS FIFTEEN MINUTES late when he slid into the booth. "Sorry. I had to make sure I wasn't being followed."

I looked him over to make sure he wasn't pulling my leg, but his face was anything but joking. He picked up the laminated menu and opened it in front of his face, though I had to believe nobody who came to this place really needed to see a menu; it was all typical diner food. He stared at the menu, silent, until the waitress came by, and then he ordered coffee and grilled cheese, same as me. She smiled at him, he smiled back and handed her the menu. As soon as she left the table, he dropped the mask.

"A woman showed up at my house at the end of the day. She said her name was Nola Lantri and it turns out she's a PI. She wanted to talk to me about Anna."

I opened my mouth to speak but didn't know what to say, so I closed it and waited.

"She said Anna is wanted in connection with a hit-and-run. She said someone died."

He was studying my face. I said nothing, moved not at all.

"I always knew Anna was running from something. All the family acted that way. I figured it was bad. I guess I'm not surprised it's this bad." Then he lifted his chin and hardened his eyes. "But I would still help her, like I did, like our family did. She's sick—very sick. You know that." He paused but still I said nothing, did not even nod my head. "If they threw her in jail she would die—but not right away. She would suffer a lot first. Maybe some people think that's what she deserves for what she did."

He kept looking at me. This was my cue to ask why he was telling me this. If I had no prior connection to Anna, the way I was pretending all along, I should have said something. Instead I waited.

Finally he said what I'd been waiting for. "That lady, Nola, also asked me if I had seen someone named Emery James—'goes by Emjay,' she said. Seems like this Emjay knew the boy who died. Seems like Nola was warning me that Emjay might be out for revenge or something."

A terrible déjà vu hit me right then: the feeling that Kip was judging me against his will. He always wanted to see me as a good person, but he constantly had to reconcile that with some of my less-than-good qualities. It wasn't Kip judging me now; it was Fernando. And why should Fernando be judging me? He was the one harboring a fugitive from the law. Yet Fernando believed in what he was doing, while I . . . I was having doubts. But how would I convey any of this to him?

I lowered my eyes, then my head, but Fernando caught my chin in his hand and lifted it. "You know what I think? I think this Emjay had plenty of chances to get her revenge already. If she hasn't done anything by now, she won't. So I told Nola I didn't know Emjay." He shrugged, and a smile played on his lips. "That was a lie. I think I do know her, at least a little."

I almost smiled back, but emotions roiled inside me. Part of me still wanted revenge. Part of me felt that Fernando was wrong, or at least too biased to be a fair judge. Anna had committed a crime, a serious one that could not be undone. She'd killed someone, and not entirely by accident. That she was mentally ill seemed mostly beside the point; that she would suffer in a way not connected to her crime was irrelevant. She had to pay.

But I wasn't the one who could make her pay. Having eased some of her suffering, there was no way I could bring her back to it.

I said cautiously, "If Nola found you and she's suspicious of me, then she's closing in. I think . . . you might need to move Anna."

He nodded. "That's what my uncles are saying. They're thinking of taking her away to …"

"No." I held up my hand right in front of his face. Fernando looked surprised. "Don't tell me. Just don't. You might trust me but . . . I'm not always sure I trust myself."

"OK, but . . . there's one more thing. Anna wants to see Grayson one more time."

It figured. She couldn't just get out of my life forever without making things extra complicated. "Nola is watching Grayson. If Anna goes to see him, Nola might show up."

"Maybe . . . maybe one of us can try to draw Nola away, get her to follow us. Then the other can bring Anna to see him."

It was just what I'd been thinking, but I hesitated to say it because I knew the logical person for each task, and I knew what that meant. "Nola seems to be following you, not me. I guess that means you should lead her off."

"Yes. And you will take Anna."

The way he was looking at me, I knew he was also saying, I *trust* you.

12

SOMETIMES WONDERED WHAT HAPPENED to Sarah Coyle after she disappeared. I tried to imagine her becoming some kind of modern-day (at least for her time) superhero, going around doing vigilante justice stuff, helping the oppressed, fighting evil. I suppose that's possible, given her character. I thought about doing some research about her, hunting down archived newspapers. But I had a feeling I would never do that, because I had a feeling Sarah Coyle hadn't become a superhero. It was easier for me to picture her living quietly and humbly and in something of a daze whenever she thought about the things she'd done, rather than being all tough and badass. Yeah, I was sure that was just me projecting, though I didn't like what it said about me. Why *wouldn't* she be a superhero? A dark, tortured one, granted, like all the best ones were, but why did I have such a hard time seeing that?

I had in the car with me that morning the woman who killed Kip. I was alone with her. I could do whatever I wanted with her, and I was taking her to see the man she loved.

I didn't know why I was doing this. Maybe I just couldn't think of any reason not to. I should have hated her, but I couldn't. That's not to say I felt all warm and fuzzy about her. I didn't *understand* her, and despite what people think, you can't really hate what you don't understand. We think that's how it goes—we think people look at someone different and don't understand why they're different so they hate the difference. But that's not quite it. What we hate is something else—maybe the fact that we can't control the person so they're more like us, so they become something we can understand. Maybe we hate our inability to understand. We're afraid and we hate the fear. Pretty soon, so that we can live with ourselves, we shift our hate to the person we think caused the whole business.

How could I hate Anna when I had no idea what was going on with her? Anna herself had no idea what was going on with her. She was crazy. She was sick. Beyond that I knew nothing, understood nothing, so I did the one thing I knew I could do: sync.

Syncing with Anna kept her calm and quiet, so from the moment I picked her up at the house (Fernando already having left, and I having checked to make sure I wasn't followed), that's what I did. She sat there next to me like we were office secretaries carpooling to work. So ordinary, so non-dramatic, except that my brain was screaming in my skull. *I could crash this car. I could drive it into a pillar and kill us both. I'm sure this piece of shit car has faulty airbags too. That would be perfect: we'd both be dead and I wouldn't have to think about how I should have been the one to die instead of Kip.* Anna looked at me with calm, blank eyes. I turned away, kept driving, kept syncing, kept screaming in my head.

I parked behind the clinic. The doctor's car wasn't where he usually parked, but I knew he'd be in eventually. A car was parked in the visitors' lot in front. It didn't match the description of the car Fernando said Nola was driving, but it could still be Nola's. This was a problem. The car could also belong to a patient, and it would be stupid for me to get so caught up in this other stuff that I neglected my job. Yet if it was Nola, I'd have failed completely by bringing Anna in. I turned to her and stopped the sync. "I need to go inside for a moment. Please wait out here."

Anna was still enjoying the momentary bliss from the sync, so she nodded—again, like we were work colleagues and I'd just told her I needed to stop at the drugstore for tampons. *You killed him*, I screamed, but I shut the car door as quietly as I could.

I entered the clinic through the back door and went out front. There was someone standing in the vestibule area that we kept unlocked so that patients could wait for us indoors if they were early and the weather was foul. It was a woman. It wasn't Nola Lantri.

I opened the door. It was Marilyn Pearson, Kip's mother.

We stared at each other, our faces mirrors of dumb-founded surprise. She recovered first, her confusion fading and a hardness closing over her. "So you've been looking for her, too," she said, her voice quiet and cold.

It took me a moment to realize "her" meant Anna, main-ly because I wasn't looking for her anymore. I nodded, not sure what to say—what even to think. This was probably Nola Lantri's mystery client. But where was Nola Lantri? Surely she couldn't have been so foolish as to just hand over the information on the whereabouts of Kip's killer to Kip's *mother*. "Did you hire a PI?" I asked.

She nodded. "The police told me they found the car, but that was all. So I tried to find her myself. I found a private investigator who actually knows her—I saw their names to-gether in a newspaper article—so I hired her."

"And . . . where is she now? I mean, the PI. Is she, uh, here with you?"

"I fired her."

"She wasn't any good?"

"No. She was very good. But I never intended for her to find Anna."

"Then why ..."

"I wanted her to get *close*. But if she actually found that *woman*"—with the sneer on her face when she said "wom-an" she might as well have said "vermin"—"she'd turn her in to the police. I won't stand for that."

I had a pretty good idea what Mrs. Pearson wanted—the same thing I'd wanted for a long time. "How did you . . . I mean, how come you're *here?*"

Marilyn Pearson should have been asking me the same question, but she didn't seem to care why I was there. Her look of determination suggested total focus on why she was there. "In her last report she told me she'd questioned this Dr. Bryant person who was very close to that *woman* and might know where she is. She also found yet another relative and questioned him. All the relatives she'd talked to before were dead ends, though. I thought this doctor was the one to watch."

My head was in spin cycle. "So . . . then you fired her?"

Marilyn nodded. "I told her she wasn't moving fast enough." She made a dismissive "hmmph" sound. "She was surprised and angry, but I did her a favor. This way she won't be responsible for what happens." Now she narrowed her eyes at me. "Nor will *you.* This is my business to take care of, not yours, so you can just leave now." The hardness in her face was also in her voice, though this time it wasn't directed at me. I'd misjudged her to just about the nth degree, in believing her too selfish to care about anyone else.

"Marilyn, wait. What are you ..."

"This man knows where the murderer is. He is going to take me to her."

"But what if he doesn't ..."

"Get out of here. You don't need to be involved in this.

This is about my son. You think *you* suffered from his loss? Your feelings are nothing compared to mine." OK, so I hadn't entirely misjudged her—she was still self-absorbed to the last—but of course she had a point. Kip was her son. What parent wouldn't want to avenge their child's murder?

We were still standing in the doorway. I hadn't moved to let her in, partly because of a clear awareness that I should definitely not let her in but also because I felt paralyzed. "Marilyn, he might not know. And . . . it might not be her."

Her eyes narrowed to slits again and I felt some of the old contempt seethe from her. "What do you know? Nothing. It's her. Get out of my way."

"It was her car. That's probably what you were told, right? The police said they identified her car, but not her. They don't know who was driving."

"GET OUT OF MY WAY."

"Yes, Emjay, why don't you get out of her way?"

Anna stood a few feet behind me. Her voice was calm, but in her face I saw...something else, not quite weariness, but maybe resignation. She wasn't afraid to face Marilyn, or me, or anyone else, I guess because we were nothing to the other demons she faced.

Marilyn barreled into me, pushing herself into the clinic, closing the door behind her. She pulled out a gun from her coat pocket and clicked off the safety.

When I look back at that moment I wonder why I did what I did. It would have been easy to do nothing at all, to let

Marilyn Pearson avenge her son's death by shooting Anna. I would get what I wanted—revenge—without putting myself at risk, and Marilyn would get what she wanted while almost certainly receiving the kind of lenience given to a middle-class, middle-age white woman avenging her son's death. Hell, with a good lawyer, she might even get off on some variation of an insanity plea—though she'd hardly be able to live any kind of satisfying life after going through all that. But at that moment I wasn't thinking. My knee-jerk instinct was to sync Marilyn Pearson so that she wouldn't shoot Anna.

"NO!" Marilyn shrieked. "I know what you're doing! That thing Kip does." *Does?* Kip had been dead for a year. "I keep telling him not to do it. His goddamned grandfather . . . I told him not to. Stop it. STOP."

The enraged contortions in her face began to relax. Slowly the tension in her body eased. She took a deep breath and released it, like a sigh.

I sighed with her.

Someone was standing behind Marilyn then, arms around her in a loose embrace, gently removing the gun from her hands. It was the doctor.

I could have yanked the gun away from him. Maybe—and I review this moment in my head again and again as well—I should have. But I let him take the gun while I continued the sync with Marilyn.

Grayson held the gun in both hands and clicked on the safety. Then he looked up and locked eyes with Anna.

"*Mi amor*," Anna whispered. There was a hint of trembling in her voice.

"Anna." There was none in Grayson's. He spoke the way he would speak to a patient: kind and caring, but as a professional.

She must have picked that up, because her face changed, flickered with pain the way it did when I first saw her in that house. Then she smiled, and began to move slowly toward him.

Grayson stood completely still. What could he do? Pointing the gun at her was useless, and they both knew it. I knew it too.

I had a choice. I could break the sync with Marilyn and try to go after Anna.

But I didn't move either.

At that point, oddly, I wondered if there would be a time later in my life when I would regret that decision—or, more likely, rationalize it. I told myself that there was nothing more I could do for Anna, but Marilyn I might still be able to help. When I look back now, I wonder: was this the truth, or was I just tired of the whole drama? I don't know. Regardless, I stayed with Marilyn.

Anna smiled and took the gun from Grayson as simply as she might take a glass of wine he was holding out for her. She held his empty hand for a moment and then released it.

Then she brought the gun up, clicked off the safety and fired.

Everyone, all four of us, fell to the floor at once.

Two of us sat up. Me first, then Marilyn, with my help. The sync was broken, of course, but she still remained comfortably spaced out.

Anna and the doctor remained down.

The doctor lay face down, his arms extended toward Anna, hands clenched into fists.

I crawled over to the doctor, knelt beside him, hesitantly put a hand on his back. He was shaking.

Anna was dead, the top of her head blown to the back of the room.

The doctor lifted his head, began clawing at the floor as though trying to get to her—or away from her? I tried to help him up, but he whispered hoarsely, "No. I need to do this myself."

Do what? Was he going to take her trace or was he trying to resist it?

The doctor got up on his knees, swaying a bit. His eyes opened, fixed on Anna, and his body went completely still.

And then someone was lifting me up, pulling me away from the doctor, pulling me outside. "Fernando?" I said, and then I choked a bit. I should have been calling for Kip.

It wasn't Kip, obviously, nor was it Fernando. Some guy I'd never even seen before was taking me outside. "Come on. Let's get you out of here. I called 911; they'll be here soon."

"The doctor . . . the gun . . . I need to help."

"You can't."

Marilyn Pearson was already outside, still standing in a bit of a daze, though the pleasant glow of it was wearing off. I guessed this guy had pulled her out first. Finally I twisted free from his grasp and turned to look at him—just an ordinary guy, skinny, pale, maybe mid-20s—and said, "Who the hell are you?"

He straightened up. "I'm Eric Lafferty. I work with Nola Lantri."

I stared at him for what seemed like about ten minutes but was probably only that many seconds. "Who knew? She really did have 'associates' after all." I laughed, a hard sound, because it was either that or start sobbing.

NOLA LANTRI HAD NOT been a dummy. Once Marilyn Pearson fired her, the PI figured the woman would act on her own—and would most likely go after one of the last two people Nola had interrogated. She had this Eric guy follow the doctor while she followed Fernando, in part to continue to search for Anna but also in case Marilyn showed up. Unfortunately, Eric Lafferty had gotten a lot more than he bargained for, as neither of them could have anticipated how things would turn out—that I would be there or that I would have brought Anna.

Nola Lantri told me this after we each gave our statements to the police, me and her and the doctor and Mrs.

Pearson. Here's the funny thing, though: she made it clear, in so many words, that this was not quite the story she'd told the police. "They were told that Marilyn had not ever made any threats to Anna or Grayson that I was aware of." She looked me dead in the eye in case I didn't get it. "She hired me simply because she needed to feel like progress was being made toward finding the person who killed her son so that this person could be apprehended and prosecuted."

The story was true enough and would never get her accused of perjury, but its omissions made it seem less likely that Marilyn Pearson would be charged with anything serious. Hell, the way the justice system works, they'd probably give her something along the lines of a parking ticket for the concealed weapon.

I didn't have a problem with that. The cynical side of me thought Nola was covering her ass, since after all it was her former client who provided the weapon that ended up killing Anna, and ethically she shouldn't have taken on a client who was very likely to commit a crime. But I could see something Nola Lantri must have seen as well: Marilyn Pearson was a different person now. The rage was gone, yet she hadn't fallen into despair. Kip's mother left the police station alone, refusing (though not in a mean way) my offer to accompany her, and while sorrow was written in her posture, there was a determination in her movements that suggested she was also moving on. Anna's suicide had ended the need for revenge, and perhaps the syncing had allowed Marilyn to realize it was possible to heal. I hoped so; she'd suffered enough.

The one person who might not agree was Fernando. Marilyn had threatened to kill a member of his family, after all, and even if Anna was not even close to being an innocent victim, Marilyn's threatening behavior could still be considered a criminal act. Would he and his family still want her prosecuted? They'd be fools if they did; what jury would convict a woman confronting her son's killer, even with a gun in her hand? Another question weighed on me: Would Fernando be angry at me for protecting Marilyn Pearson? Of course that would be blatant hypocrisy, but he still might feel the need for someone to pay, however misguidedly (and I knew all about that), for Anna's death. Anyway, why should it matter what he thought of me? Chances were I'd never see him again.

There was one person I absolutely had to see again, and that was the doctor. He knew it as well as I did, and as soon as I saw Marilyn off, I turned to see him leaning against a car, waiting for me. I approached him immediately. "Coffee?" he asked with a tired half smile.

I nodded, and he gestured at the café across the street.

We ordered and sat in silence for a while. I didn't feel the need to make idle chatter, but we couldn't sit there forever without saying a word. Finally the doctor spoke first.

"I can provide you paid leave for however long you need, Emery, and then if you're willing, I hope you'll consider coming back to the clinic to work."

It wasn't something I'd expected him to say right away; although I'd felt relief that Marilyn Pearson appeared ready to move on, with the doctor it seemed wrong. "Where's the clinic going to be?" I blurted.

It was the first question that came to my head, and though at first it seemed even to me like a strange one, I realized exactly why I'd asked it. The answer mattered. The doctor knew why it mattered. Instead of looking puzzled, he looked me in the eye and said, "It will still be there in the same place."

"That's not all that'll still be there. How are you going to do this? How are you going to go in every day knowing this was where she died? How ..." I left unspoken the question, how about her trace?

The doctor said nothing. I had my answer: he had already gotten her trace. He'd gone back to the way he was before I'd met him.

"You know you'll end up like her."

"Maybe she was the one who ended up like me."

I slammed down my cup. "That's crap. Stop talking in riddles. Anna went crazy and killed herself because of her addiction to trace. She thought you were stronger than that; she thought you had overcome it."

"She certainly put that theory to the test, didn't she."

"You wanted her to be like you once, right? So you could share something? Well, maybe she wanted you to be like her. She wanted you to suffer."

"Turnabout is fair play."

"Shut the fuck up." Now he was really surprised—and listening, I hoped. "You admitted that what you did was wrong, getting Anna addicted like you were. You tried to atone. Great. Well, what Anna did was wrong too and she atoned for it too. And now that's all over. You can't do the work you want to do if you're back to doing that trace shit."

He actually smiled at that point. "This isn't meth, Emery."

"So what? Looked how it fucked up Anna. That's going to be you, Bryant."

It was the first time I'd called him by his name. He wasn't "the doctor," said in reverential tones; he was just another messed up person I knew. "What does Nola Lantri think about all this?" I added.

That made him smile in a different way—bitterly. "Nola Lantri likely figures I've never changed. I daresay she'd have bet money on this particular outcome—my going back to taking trace—if such a thing were possible."

"Well, why can't you prove her wrong?"

"What, and deprive her of the chance to be smug at my expense?"

He was joking but there was no lightness in it, no spirit. I knew there was no point in my staying to argue with him—it was too late, had been from the moment Anna died.

I stood up to leave, but Grayson Bryant had one more thing to say. "You could have stopped her, you know."

There was no malice in the accusation; he sounded like someone simply pointing out an interesting observation: I could have stopped Anna from killing herself. He didn't need to sound malicious; it was a thought that had been weighing on me even before he'd stated it, though for very mixed reasons. Anna was sick and needed help; now she couldn't get it. Anna had committed a terrible crime and hadn't been brought to justice for it; now she never would be.

But there was another way to look at that accusation: I could have stopped Anna by killing her myself. And still another: I could have let Marilyn kill Anna. I didn't do either of those things, and those thoughts were weighing on me too.

I leaned toward him like someone about to whisper a secret. "Yes, I could have stopped her. You could have resisted taking her trace. Now we have to live with that. You're ahead of me on that score; you seem to be living with it just fine."

I left him there, left the café and stepped outside with no clear idea where I was going next.

A WEEK LATER FERNANDO asked to meet me at the Houghton Diner. I'm not sure how he got my phone number— hell, maybe now he was hiring Nola Lantri—but I didn't much care or mind. I wanted to see him, so I agreed.

A booth in a diner, grilled cheese and coffee, a boy and a girl. It sounded sweet and lovely but was mostly just incredibly tense, and not in the cute first-date way. This wasn't a date, after all. This was . . . well, I don't think either of us knew.

"I'm sorry about Anna," I said right away. I hadn't said that to the doctor—there seemed no need for that formality—but I wanted to say it to Fernando and wanted him to know I meant it.

He nodded. "Thanks." After a moment, he added, "So . . . I guess the clinic is closed, huh. What are you going to do? I guess you're out of a job."

I didn't want to get into the conversation I'd had with the doctor, so I just shrugged. "I'll find something else."

"What about med school? Become a doctor yourself?"

Now I frowned; I didn't think Fernando knew that much about my past, the fact that I'd once been in med school. "Nope. Not for me."

He made a derisive snorting sound, shaking his head. "Wow. 'Not for me.' You can choose that. Privilege is amazing."

I didn't know if he was joking, but I got riled anyway. "*Privilege*? Are you fucking kidding me? You think I'm some spoiled rich white girl? I put myself through a year of premed *on my own*, no handouts from *nobody*."

"You didn't finish med school."

I felt another flash of ire, but he was just stating a fact. "Yeah, I didn't finish, but not because I didn't want to work to pay my way. I just . . . didn't have any reason to keep going."

Fernando shook his head. "That's even worse, then. You couldn't even find a reason to do something that worthwhile?"

I smiled grimly. "Yeah, that's worse. But you're just as bad. Why don't you go to med school if you think it's so amazing? Let me guess: you can't afford it, right? That's not legit. That's an excuse. You can do it just as well as I could; lots of people can. There are ways."

As soon as I said that, I remembered one of the "ways" Kip and I had used. All so unnecessary, I thought now. If we hadn't . . . but there was no reason to go down that road. It was as pointless as the road Marilyn Pearson had gone down.

I glanced at Fernando, who had been quiet while I'd been recalling memories I wished I didn't have but still, for the past year, had been loath to let go of. He was grinning faintly. "Ways, huh. You think you can show me some of those ways?"

Good lord, was I *blushing*? There wasn't anything terribly suggestive in what he said, but how he said it—definitely something there.

"Actually," I prattled, "there is a way I can make some money, but it's totally nuts. Nola Lantri asked me if I wanted to work for her. Can you believe that?" I laughed to emphasize, perhaps a bit too forcedly, my disdain for the offer.

Fernando did not laugh. He peered quizzically at me. "Why is that funny? Do you think it would take up too much time?"

"Nah, it's not that. It would be all, like, part-time contract stuff, but come on. It would be like living in some lame TV series."

"But it's not a TV series. It's your life. You can do a lot of good things with it."

"It's too hard to do good things all the time. Right now I'd settle for just not doing anything bad."

Fernando smiled. "First do no harm. Isn't that the first part of the doctor's oath?"

I was not smiling. "I'm not a doctor, Fernando. I'm not a saint either."

"Nobody is. But you still can do good things. You helped Anna when she needed it most."

That surprised me. Far from blaming me for not saving her, Fernando was praising me. I liked the praise but it made me uncomfortable. It was praise I didn't deserve. "Believe me," I said quietly, "I could just as easily have gone the other way."

And even though I had once thought of this as Kip's story and mine, I told him about Sarah Coyle.

Afterwards, we sat in silence for a few minutes. The waitress came, refilled our coffees, left. Finally Fernando spoke. "Sarah Coyle took extreme revenge. You took extreme mercy. Neither one of those things is going to be easy to understand. If you'd done like Sarah Coyle, you might spend the rest of your life wondering why you turned yourself into a person more willing and able to cause pain than anything else. As it is …"

"Yeah, as it is . . . what? I spend the rest of my life wondering why I froze? Why I was such a goddamn coward?"

He shrugged. "Maybe." That surprised me; I'd expected him to say I wasn't a coward, the way people always do in that knee-jerk, utterly pointless fashion. "Funny thing, though. It's usually other people who will call someone a coward. When it's us, we know damn well why we did what we did, and we'd probably do it the same way again even if we don't want to admit it. If you care too much that people will think you're a coward, that's cowardly. If you don't care what other people think, then it doesn't matter. You did what you did. You had reasons. That's all."

That seemed way too simplistic, but I could see what he meant, and I was glad he was saying it—something nice, something positive—rather than the things I'd thought he'd be saying.

And then I compared it to the last thing Grayson Bryant had said to me: You could have stopped her. He was right; I could have synced Anna and kept her from firing the gun. I didn't, and I had to live with my choice, but I would be the one figuring out how to do that. It had been my decision. That mattered.

We both tucked into our sandwiches then, lightening up a bit and acting like normal people in a diner. As we ate, I glanced at him a few times. If our lives hadn't been so fucked up, who knows, maybe we'd leave the diner together and go back to my place and tear into each other all night. The thought made me smile, and when I looked up and saw an identical smile on his face, I knew he'd probably had the same thought.

But I went home alone. Fernando didn't seem too disappointed; he was a guy after all, a hot one, and I suppose he had enough confidence to believe that this wasn't over yet. It probably wasn't over—but it also wasn't what I needed right then.

Back in my shithole apartment alone, I surveyed the grimness of my life—the sparse possessions, the lack of a sense of rootedness, of belonging—and shrugged. And then laughed at myself for shrugging when no one was there to see it. Filling the emptiness with a body would work for one night—maybe more, the way it had with Kip—but it wouldn't last. I'd always had a lot of disdain for girls who lived and died for a boy's approval; at best they ended up unhappy and at worst, well, you name it. With Kip, though, I wasn't interested in his approval so much as his ability to make me judge myself fairly, to weigh my more selfish impulses against the things I knew I should do because they were right.

I sat on the worn futon sofa and picked up Kip's books, all I had left of him—all, that is, except the person I'd become. I wanted to believe that even without Kip I could still weigh the good and bad sides of myself and come out the better for it, because he'd helped me get here.

I held the books for a while, and then I got up and put them up on a bookshelf. There was nothing else on the shelf—they looked a bit lonely there—but I wanted them in a place where they wouldn't get lost.

I didn't know if I would ever see any of those people again, Fernando or the doctor, Nola Lantri or Mrs. Pearson, or what was going to happen in my life in general. That didn't matter. I knew that however other people saw me, they were seeing a person who was winning the battle against herself—by herself.

ACKNOWLEDGMENTS

Thanks to Mary Maddox for your hard work and guidance, The Quality Writers (Jeff Kohmstedt and Dan Davis) for your input on early versions of *Vibe/Sync*, and Ken Welle for everything you do.

ABOUT THE AUTHOR

Letitia L. Moffitt was born and raised in Hawaii. She received a doctoral degree in English/Creative Writing from Binghamton University. Her first novel, *Sidewalk Dancing*, was published by Atticus Books in November 2013. Her novel *Trace*—Book 1 of the TraceWorld series—was published by Cantraip Press in March 2015. In her spare time Moffitt runs ultramarathons and blogs about her experiences at http://letitiamoffitt.blogspot.com.